The Paper Man and Other Stories

William Thompson

Copyright © 2015 William Thompson
All rights reserved.

ISBN: 1507568975
ISBN 13: 9781507568972
Library of Congress Control Number: 2015900783
CreateSpace Independent Publishing Platform
North Charleston, South Carolina

For my parents
Anne and Don

ACKNOWLEDGMENTS

I wish to thank the Alberta Arts Foundation for its generous financial support early in the writing of these short stories. I also want to thank all those people who read and commented on these stories over the years, and those who kindly purchased them as Kindle e-texts. A special thanks to Tom Wharton for some detailed and keen insights into the collection in its final stages. Most of all, I want to acknowledge my children, who have demonstrated an unwavering and lifelong belief in me as a writer and storyteller.

TABLE OF CONTENTS

Acknowledgments	v
Teddy	1
The Man with the Plastic Face	12
My Brother's Keeper	22
China Dolls	34
Martie	40
Scavengers	47
Transformations	62
Tracks	75
Tiff	84
The End of Summer	93
A Visit to the Calgary Zoo	101
The Paper Man	109
The Tent Trailer	126
Afterword	133

TEDDY

What Molly wanted to remember about that summer was Teddy standing on the roof in a lightning storm, an upright figure dressed only in a pair of cutoffs, laughing and waving his arms as the lightning branched above his head and the rain poured down. That had been just one of those stupid things Teddy had done. Once she was no longer angry, the scene stayed with Molly. Later, much later, she would dream of it, and it became one of those memories she would take out, looking at it as she would a photograph in an old family album.

The eaves on the front of the house had gotten clogged. That night they had been out for dinner, leaving the three kids at home with Tammy in charge. The thunder and lightning had started while they were in the restaurant. It was an Indian place. Molly had wanted to try something different, and Teddy, as ever, was willing to try something new. They heard the thunder halfway through dinner. Molly got up to call the kids from the phone booth in the lobby.

"They're fine," she said when she came back to the table. "Alex is scared, but Tammy's reading to him."

"What about Josh?"

"He's fine, too. He thinks the lightning is cool."

On the way home the two of them became increasingly quiet, Molly driving determinedly through the sheeting rain, while Teddy sat staring out the passenger window. They arrived back at the house to find water pouring off the roof and splashing down onto the walk in front of the door.

"I'll have to do something about that," said Teddy, staring up at the fall of water from the roof.

"What?" asked Molly, looking at him and having to raise her voice to be heard above the wind and rain.

"I have to do something—about the water," he shouted. "I'm going to change."

Molly went into the house and talked to the kids, gathering up Alex and hugging Tammy with her free arm.

"Did you see the waterfall?" asked Josh excitedly. "We have a waterfall on our front step!"

Teddy came out of their bedroom dressed in nothing but a pair of old cutoffs. "I'll be back," he said.

"Put on your gardening shoes," called Molly.

"I want to come!" called Josh.

"No!" said Molly. "Watch your father from the window if you have to."

Teddy got the ladder and climbed onto the roof. When he didn't come back after fifteen minutes, Molly grabbed an umbrella and went outside. She walked out to the yard to look up to the roof. The faces of the kids were all pressed to the front window. On the roof, Teddy stood and waved at her. He had cleared the eaves so the water no longer poured onto the step. Now he stood, arms uplifted and waving in the rain. Lightning lit the lower clouds and thunder echoed around the sky, illuminating the figure of Teddy, laughing and waving with the lightning branching behind him.

When they'd first met, Teddy was writing for weeklies. He, like Molly, was a small-town kid, but he never minded the moving-around lifestyle of a weeklies reporter. Both of them finished high school but neither went to university. Molly had thought about a community college in the city, but there were jobs in those days, and it was easy to make money, hang on to it if you were smart, and then buy a house.

Teddy, on the other hand, was lousy with money. He always had been. He never drank it away like so many people Molly knew or had heard about from high school, but he was generous with his credit card and always made just the minimum payment, saying he'd pay it off the next month. You couldn't do that very long before you had a bill big enough to choke a horse. He was a risk that way, but Molly thought she could manage him.

She had decided to marry Teddy in a lightning storm. They were in Calgary on a weekend in July, and they decided at midnight to drive back to Edmonton. Molly's mother had just gone into the hospital. It wasn't an emergency: Rachel had been waiting for hip surgery for months, but Molly was anxious anyway. They had been going to wait until the next day to drive back, but Teddy insisted he wasn't tired, so off they went.

The storm caught up to them outside Red Deer, on that long and seemingly interminable stretch of highway that runs between Red Deer and Edmonton. There had been drought for a couple of years, but that didn't stop the lightning storms. It was spectacular, driving along the highway, the flashes lighting the sky from horizon to horizon, tearing the world with explosions of sound that shook the car—but not a drop of rain, just the lightning, the thunder, and Teddy looking over at her occasionally and laughing. He loved it.

It hadn't really been the storm that had decided Molly, but Teddy's willingness to respond to her anxiety about her mother. The lightning storm had just fixed it in her mind.

After they'd arrived in the city, grabbed breakfast at an all-night diner, and then gone to her mom's, Molly had made her decision. Molly's parents had decided to retire in Edmonton. They sold the farm and bought a house in town. Within a year, her father was dead, and Molly's mother was on her own. Molly had a key to Rachel's house. Teddy slept for a while in an overstuffed armchair in the living room while Molly considered. She told him as they drove up to the hospital.

"I want to marry you," Molly said, staring out the window at the passing stream of storefronts, car lots, and fast-food joints. When he didn't say anything right away, she stole a glance at him.

He had a sort of half smile on his face, and that dreamy expression that Molly had come to almost envy. She always wondered where he went when he looked like that. Then he came back to himself and looked at her. "Sure," he said. And that was it.

Not a terribly romantic beginning. Being married to Teddy was at times exasperating and infuriating. Fights tended to begin with Molly screaming and end in long silences that could last for days. Teddy would sometimes forget to tell her things about the schedule, about the house, and even the kids; but he always managed to surprise her in small ways that made Molly remember in the end why she loved him. Teddy tried. He always tried. But it was an inescapable fact that Teddy Richards was never going to succeed at life.

Teddy was a good reporter while it lasted. They moved to the city, and he got a job with the CBC. It looked good for a few years. Teddy did all right, and Molly didn't worry over much. Bills tended to mount, but that's what happened when you had two kids and a mortgage.

Then the cuts at the station. Teddy never had enough seniority to hang on to his job, and interest rates hit the roof. Molly was terrified they would lose the house. But they had a fixed mortgage that protected them for the moment, and Teddy never stopped getting jobs. Everyone Molly knew had a story about being unemployed or losing a house. And then Molly got pregnant with Alex. What a time to get pregnant. Molly thought for about a week that she would lose her mind.

"I'm pregnant," she said to Teddy one morning before the kids were up. Teddy was at the counter, putting together yogurt and granola. He looked at her. His face was lined and hardened now—just part of the change she had noticed in him since their marriage began. For a moment, Molly thought he was going to blame her, ask her why the hell she hadn't kept better track. Wasn't it the woman's responsibility to keep track? Oh god.

But Teddy's expression slid into that dreamy half smile that she hadn't seen in a long time. She didn't want to see it now. She wanted to hit him, scream at him, make him understand how difficult this was going to be.

Teddy reached out and gently took her face into his hands. He kissed her forehead and then her eyes. She could smell coffee on his soft breath.

"I love you," he whispered. She could feel his lips speaking the words against her forehead.

And it was all right again for a while—all right in the middle of all the wondering about jobs, about the house, about too many bills.

But no one starved, as Molly's mother always said. Molly learned to be creative in how she spent money on groceries and clothes. She combed the bargain stores, swallowing her pride as she went through the racks at the Goodwill. Everyone was fed and clothed, and the kids generally happy. Teddy worked two and sometimes three jobs, which Molly found hard. But even tired as he was, Teddy spent time with the kids, reading to them, wrestling on the floor with them, and taking Tammy out on long bike rides.

Molly saved what she could for Christmas and Easter. She did what she could for her mother, dragging the boys along until it was just Alex after Josh had started school. When Alex was three, Molly got the job at the hospital. Molly had no illusions why. One of the two people on the hiring committee was the cousin of a friend. Nevertheless, it had been hard to go back to work full-time, but nine years at home raising kids was about enough. Teddy was, of course, supportive. He arranged his schedule so he could get the kids to school and Alex to Rachel's. It was hard. She had been away from it for so long. But Molly had a sinking feeling that Teddy was never going to find anything that would last long, and she wanted to do something that would give her a greater sense of security. She had worried that having a full-time job might wound Teddy's pride at having to be the breadwinner, but it didn't turn out that way.

Perhaps it was something that she'd noticed in his face lately. He wasn't angry or brooding, like so many of the husbands Molly knew who couldn't find or keep a job. Teddy didn't drink too much—thank god. But it was an expression on Teddy's face she caught from time to time that pulled at her insides. He looked simply baffled. It made him appear young and vulnerable. The world wasn't going to allow Teddy to succeed in his own right. He would always be a good father and husband, but he was never going to be anything on his own terms.

Molly had to work hard not to be frustrated, not to criticize. She wanted to, but instead she encouraged him. He was able to quit one of his jobs after Molly started at the hospital. "Why don't you write?" she asked, carefully. They were lying in bed, Teddy with an arm around her neck, holding her, absently tracing the shape of her breast with a forefinger.

"Write?" he asked. His voice sounded distant in the darkness.

"Yeah," said Molly. She turned on her side to face him. "You could go back to some of those stories you wrote years ago, or write down some of the stories you tell to the kids. Or even see if you could start writing for a paper again."

"Maybe," he murmured.

His voice sounded sleepy, and he ran his hand down her side until it rested on her hip. Molly hated that spot. Teddy gently pinched her hip, and then he sighed and fell asleep.

But the look on his face didn't go away. Molly would surprise it there more and more often. But Teddy never complained; he just kept working, playing with the kids, taking his turn at making dinner or cleaning the house and yard.

After Christmas of that year Teddy's father had a stroke. Teddy hadn't spoken to his father in years, but when he answered the call from his sister in Drum, he went straight down.

"Take the car."

"I don't want to take the car."

"You'll need it."

"You'll need the car. I'll take the bus. Ellen said I could use her car. She and her husband have two."

"But…" said Molly.

"For Christ's sake, Molly. You need the car. I'll be fine."

She stood and looked at him for a moment. She felt as though a hand was clutching at her chest and belly.

"Oh shit," he said.

Teddy walked back and forth across the kitchen. Molly watched him. Then he came forward and hugged her hard. "I'm sorry. I'm sorry. This is just making me a little crazy, that's all."

Crazy, thought Molly. Teddy never acted normal when the subject of his family came up. She had a bad feeling about all of it.

Teddy made three trips to Drum. On the third trip, Teddy's dad died in the hospital. There was a fourth trip with all of them—Teddy, silent and strained, and the kids, edgy and trying not to show it. Molly held them together that time, all through the visiting, the funeral, and the explanations of why the kids had never known their grandpa Richards or any of the other people in Teddy's family.

"But why?" insisted Tammy. She looked at Molly half in resentment, half with the same expression of baffled pain that Molly so often saw on Teddy's face.

"Your dad never got along with his own father, or anyone else in his family," Molly said, carefully. "He left home as a young man and started moving around the province working for small newspapers. That's how I met him. But he never wanted to go back to his home or his family."

She knew that Tammy didn't understand, that the explanation didn't really explain. Desperate to distract her children, she took them to the dinosaur museum, where Alex and even Josh stood wide-eyed at the skeletons and pictures and displays, and Tammy stomped along behind, looking alternately tearful and resentful.

But Molly got them through that weekend and back on the road to home. At long last, they tumbled out of the car in front of the house. The days were getting longer, Molly noticed as she hustled the kids up the walk to the front door—still cold, even for March, but longer.

After settling the kids in their beds, Molly came downstairs to find Teddy sitting in the darkened kitchen. He looked at her, his face shadowed.

"He always said I was a failure," Teddy said softly.

Molly moved closer, trying to see Teddy's face in the shadows. She reached out to touch his shoulder.

"I failed my driving test three times. Did I ever tell you that? He said I was an idiot—actually, he said I was a fucking idiot. I had some money saved. I swore that once I passed that test, I was going to buy a car and leave and never go back. I did pass, and I did buy a car. I never wanted to go back."

After that night, Teddy wasn't able to have sex. Molly didn't notice it right away. There was always a lot to do, but one day Molly realized that they hadn't had sex since before the day Teddy had received the phone call about his dad. That was in late January; it was now the beginning of May.

Molly was lying in bed, listening to the sound of a robin singing his heart out in the tall spruce that stood just outside the window. She could hear Teddy moving around downstairs, the smell and sound of perking coffee drifting up to her.

She cornered him in the kitchen. She opened his robe and slid her arms around his bare chest. "I miss you," she murmured into his neck.

Teddy stroked her hair. "Yes," he said. He gently pulled away from her and retied his robe. "I can't, you know. Not anymore."

"What do you mean?" asked Molly. She suddenly felt overlarge in her bathrobe—the one she had found at the Goodwill, a steal at five dollars.

Teddy gave her a searching look. "I can't," he said again. "I can't get an erection anymore. I've tried—lots of times—but it won't happen."

Teddy reached up to the cupboard and took down two mugs. He poured coffee. "It's not you, you know. It's nothing to do with you. It's just me." He laughed, a little shakily, sipping at his coffee. "Maybe I'm done. Metaphorically gelded, so to speak." He looked at her.

"Well, you are sort of stupid," Molly said evenly. "I doubt that you are done." She reached over and stroked his face. "Give it some time."

He laughed again, but the shakiness was still there.

They took time to be with each other after that for a while. It hadn't been this way between them since she'd become pregnant with Josh. Molly was the one directing things, as she had been then. Once, before she knew for certain she was pregnant with their second, Molly grabbed Teddy's hand and started pulling him off the couch where he sat watching television.

"Again?" he asked, looking up at her almost imploringly.

Molly straddled him where he sat on the couch. She held his face in her hands. "Your wife wants to have sex with you. I suggest you don't argue."

Teddy had never really been demanding, but he had never taken much convincing, either—completely typical that way. Sometimes Molly wished that he would be more demanding, but he just wasn't. She remembered sitting around with other lactating women—women who swore over babies who bit, toddlers who insisted, and husbands who demanded.

"I tell him he has two hands," said a friend of Molly's during one of their frequent gatherings. "And he doesn't even need two hands. At the moment, I haven't got any."

Molly had laughed along with the others, sitting around one of the many living rooms. But she also remembered feeling a little sad. It had never been like that with Teddy. If anything, it had always been Molly who had to ask. Teddy took care of her, made sure of her in bed, but it was Teddy who less and less frequently had an orgasm, who had something that seemed to be slowly but relentlessly eating him alive.

And that's where things stood at the end of that summer after Teddy's dad had died. They took a short holiday to the lake. They couldn't afford anything else. Molly blamed herself afterward, but she wanted to blame Teddy more—for deserting them, for leaving her to raise three kids on her own. Sometimes, she actually hated him—the memory of him—but it didn't last. She mostly felt bad for her children, especially her baby, Alex.

In the year that followed, Molly would wake up with the scene at the lake replaying itself in her head. And sometimes she would wake to hear Tammy sobbing into her pillow, and Molly would slip out of the bed and into Tammy's room, sitting on the edge of Tammy's bed and rubbing her back, stroking her hair, and crooning to her until Tammy at long last would fall asleep.

Molly made her decision in the middle of the night the following spring. She had barely managed to keep things together these past eight months, and she knew that she couldn't do it indefinitely. She thought about it for a week, and then she called her children in to the living room, gathering them up into her arms as best she could. They were growing.

"You want to go to school?" asked Tammy, bemused.

"Adults can go to school," said Josh.

"Will you go to my school?" asked Alex.

"No," said Molly. "I'll go to a very big school called the university. But then I'll be a teacher, and then I would go to a school like yours and work in a classroom."

"You'll be my teacher?" asked Alex.

Molly laughed. The sound seemed foreign to her ears. But it was settled. Explaining to the kids why they needed to move was more difficult. There was resentment—crying and screaming and silences. But Molly was determined. It made her sad to realize it was this same determination that had driven the family for all those years.

For the next four months, Molly had less time to think, but she stopped dreaming. Even still, in the packing and cleaning that followed, she kept looking up expecting to see Teddy, filling a box or standing there looking for the next thing to do.

But Teddy was gone. He had made his decision the summer before, standing on the edge of a lake under a lowering sky, the wind tearing the tops of the waves and blowing the fine rain sideways into their faces.

They could see the overturned canoe between the breaks in the waves: a bright yellow canoe with two heads bobbing alongside. Someone had already gone for help, but Teddy was determined to do something.

He kept saying that it wasn't far. With two extra life jackets in tow, Teddy splashed into the waves, looking like a collection of orange bags as the water rose to his neck.

But the help didn't come quickly enough. The storm worsened, and the overturned canoe drifted farther and farther from shore. As it bobbed up and down between the waves, Molly kept searching for those orange life jackets, but she couldn't see them.

They found Teddy's body two days later. There had been three people in the canoe, two boys and a girl, none of whom had a life jacket, and all of whom were under sixteen. All drowned—all scattered up and down the reedy shore of the lake, bloated and discoloured after being in the water for so long. She had to make sure it was Teddy. She looked once at the bloated and purpled face, but she couldn't look again. That was the part of the nightmare that Molly wouldn't let rise through to her conscious mind.

She sometimes wondered if she had done the right thing. But now, sitting on her couch, sipping a mug of tea and looking out the window at the children playing in the courtyard, she knew she had done the right thing. University housing wasn't so bad. She and Tammy had their own rooms while Alex and Josh shared.

There was enough from the sale of the house for them to get comfortably settled. Molly breathed in the scent of lemon. She could hear Tammy singing to herself upstairs. Josh was running around with the friends he had made the day they arrived in the complex. And then there was Alex, her baby Alex, playing with the other kids in the courtyard behind this row of housing. Molly watched as he ran across the grass, arms upraised, laughing and being chased by a girl two or three years older.

It was the kindness of the people she had met since coming here that she found overwhelming—even this girl, this beautiful ten-year-old girl, with her ponytail, her laughing blue eyes, and her backward baseball cap, was happy to play with her son. She was grateful, she thought, grateful for the simple kindnesses of those who had become part of her life.

Teddy was gone. He had left an empty space in her life and her children's lives that would take time to fill. She had wept enough tears in the nights and days since to wonder if she could fill up that space. But it didn't fill. It was simply washed clean—empty and aching. And it was here, in this place while she went to school, that she was going to find a way to give herself and her children back something of what had been taken from them all, to make sense of something that made no sense, to give meaning to a space that had been thrust upon them all, a space that Molly knew, in some form or other, would probably be with them always.

THE MAN WITH THE PLASTIC FACE

Ernie's aunt Louise and uncle Tom had no kids. A couple without kids in Galahad was an odd thing, but what struck me even more than the absence of children was what Ernie told me about his uncle's plastic face, a story that held me with a morbid fascination that kept me coming back to the farm through that winter and into the spring.

The MacLaren place was about a mile and a half east of town. If there wasn't too much snow, Ernie and I would ride our bikes out to the farm. We would take the range road, arriving at the farm sweating under our parkas, our faces half-frozen from the wind that whipped over fallow fields with nothing to stop it for what seemed like a hundred miles. If we walked the train tracks instead of the road, then we would come to the house from across the pasture, our boots crunching over wind-packed snow. Apart from my own curiosity about Ernie's uncle Tom, I was never sure why we went so often, only that it wasn't home, and we were treated like guests rather than something vaguely annoying and in the way. Not that I thought about it like that at the time. Since Ernie and I mostly behaved ourselves, Ernie's aunt Louise never told us to go home, or asked us if we should be somewhere else.

Ernie and I would show up at the farm after school. On Saturday afternoons Mrs. MacLaren would usually drive into town or into the city, so we didn't bother showing up. But after school it was different. She never minded us dropping in, and she always told us to come in and talk to her while she made dinner. It probably didn't hurt that Ernie could charm his aunt simply by looking at her with those big green eyes. He acted the clown and made her laugh until she turned pink, while she kept coming with the cookies, or squares, or whatever else she had been baking that day. I liked Ernie's aunt, but his uncle Tom was a different matter. He had that plastic face—at least that's what Ernie told me—and I always felt a little unnerved by, and drawn to, this man who had supposedly lost half his face in some farming accident.

I mostly saw Mr. MacLaren at a distance. Sometimes he would come into the house while we were there after school. He would leave his boots and jacket on the porch and come silently into the kitchen, carrying the smell of outside—of cold wind and straw and manure. Ernie and I would look at each other, and he always made a face as though he were going to gag whenever he thought his uncle wasn't looking. I always sank as low as possible into my chair once Mr. MacLaren came into the kitchen, but Ernie would talk to his uncle in the same breezy way he had with his aunt. Mr. MacLaren never said much. He would grunt at us, and then go and pour himself a coffee from the pot at the back of the stove, which Mrs. MacLaren always had ready when he came through the door.

Tom MacLaren was not a tall man, and he didn't look much like a farmer. He had narrow, fine-boned hands and must have been shorter even than my own father, but he gave the impression of size, and when he came into the room, the kitchen didn't seem big enough to hold him. Coming in from outside on those cold winter days, the right side of his face would be red and glowing but less so the left, paling to fish-belly white toward his left eye and the thick scar that ran from hair to jawline. The left side of his face was plastic—at least that was what Ernie said—but I could never believe everything that Ernie told me.

Ernie said his uncle had fallen face-first into a combine when he was a young man. "Just fell right in. Chewed his face to rat shit so there was hardly anything left."

This was on a day in March, after Ernie had taken me to the farm half a dozen times. We were riding our bikes. Snow still clung to the sides of roads and sheltered spots, and the wind, fresh and cold, blew the surfaces of the meltwater into tiny ripples.

"No joke," said Ernie. "Went off to Philadelphia to get himself a new face—new eye, too."

"What? Just like that? You're full of shit," I said.

"No, peckerhead! You think you can just get on a plane and fly someplace when you got just half a face? It was some kind of ambulance thing."

"Then why didn't he go to Edmonton?" I asked, not really wanting to give him the point.

Ernie hooted. "Edmonton!" he said. "You can't go to Edmonton for something like that! Edmonton's just a shit town in the middle of nowhere. You got to go to the big city if you want a new face."

"And a new eye?"

"And a new eye," Ernie said expansively. "They make 'em the same way they make false teeth."

I wasn't sure what Ernie meant about the false teeth, but I let it go. He was riding close beside me, and we were pedaling down the center of the road.

"And," said Ernie, dropping his voice, "he can take it off. Take it right off, so you can see all the bones and veins and stuff underneath." He gave another great, hooting laugh and pedaled off down the road.

I didn't believe the part about Mr. MacLaren taking off his face, but it was enough to give me the creeps, thinking of him as some kind of mangled zombie out of a horror picture.

The next couple of times I saw Mr. MacLaren I watched him closely, but he never looked much different from anyone else, even for supposedly having a plastic face. He never smiled; apparently, he couldn't smile with the left side of his face, so he never smiled at all. He didn't say much, either, and never noticed Ernie and me unless we happened to get in his way, which was something we tried to avoid.

It went on like that, through the end of March and into April. After school, as the days lengthened, we would ride out to the farm. The kitchen was always neat and clean, even when Mrs. MacLaren had spent what must have been the whole day baking. Sometimes we came closer to supper, and still the kitchen was always neat and tidy—no stacks of dirty dishes or unwashed pots cluttering the stove—and the floor was so clean I felt afraid to walk on it.

The thing I remember most from that kitchen was the smell. It smelled of cooking and baking and coffee, something always in the oven or on the stove—steaming, hissing, or bubbling. The only time my own house smelled like that was at Christmas. Mrs. MacLaren herself looked as neat and tidy as her kitchen. She never wore makeup, but she always looked nice, as though nothing at all could knock her out of sorts, as my own mother would say when there were too many things to do in too short a time.

But Mr. and Mrs. MacLaren didn't have any kids, which no doubt made their lives easier. I wondered why. I sometimes thought that if I had a choice of whom I would have picked for my mother, it would have been Mrs. MacLaren. I'd gotten it into my head that winter that maybe my own parents weren't, after all, my real parents, and I couldn't stop thinking about it. Mrs. MacLaren seemed just like a mom, but even at the time I wondered if she was that way precisely because she had no kids of her own.

Their lack of children was one point that Ernie was not prepared to discuss. He never mentioned it, and once when I asked him, he refused to be drawn out.

"Some people don't want to have kids. What the hell is wrong with that?"

We were walking along the tracks, each of us balanced on a rail. Ernie's tone was surly, but I persisted.

"Yeah," I countered, "but your aunt does. You can tell."

"Maybe, but Uncle Tom doesn't. He can't stand kids."

"He doesn't seem to mind us so much," I pointed out. "If he can't stand kids, then why doesn't he just tell us to bugger off?"

"You think you're so goddamn smart." Ernie's face was red. "Just drop it, okay!"

I dropped it—for the moment, anyway. I couldn't handle people getting mad at me, even Ernie. Every now and then I would try to raise the subject, but Ernie would just glare at me until I stopped asking questions.

But I couldn't let it go. One evening, I asked my mom about Mr. and Mrs. MacLaren. She was pulling the roasting pan out of the oven. Her face was flushed, and her hair was coming out in long strands from the bun that she always tied at the back of her neck.

"Why don't they have any kids?" she asked in the absent way that told me she was only half listening. I had to ask again before she even looked at me. She shoved the pan back into the oven and set the pot holders on the counter.

"Why don't they have any kids?" she said again. "Toby, why on Earth do you want to know?"

"I don't know," I muttered. I looked down and shoved my thumb at the account books spread over the table. My mom looked after the books for the garage, and she had been doing month-end while getting supper ready. "I just wondered. It's weird they don't have kids. They aren't old or anything."

She came over to the table and sat down. I had her full attention now, and I was beginning to squirm as she looked at me across the table. I got her full attention only when I was in trouble, like the time I pasted a happy face sticker onto the top of my nightstand. I tried to get it off with my pocket knife, but all I managed to do was gouge lines into the wood. I remembered, too late, that my grandpa had built that nightstand, and my mother was just about as mad as I could remember when she discovered what I did.

"Ernie's aunt Louise can't have any children, Toby," my mother said, still looking at me across the table. "She had a hysterectomy about five years ago. That's an operation to remove a woman's uterus."

I would have given anything to get away from the table in that moment, but my mother had me pinned to my chair with her eyes. "Oh," I mumbled.

Maybe Ernie knew and maybe he didn't, but I felt weird around Ernie after that. It was like sharing a secret to which I had no right.

Around the middle of April, a week before the Easter weekend, I went to the farm on my own. Ernie seemed less interested in going, and every time I asked him he would just shrug it off.

"Jesus! Go yourself," he finally said to me. "I don't feel like going there." He didn't explain why.

On Saturday, I got my bike and headed out to the farm. Ernie had gone with his dad to Viking, and I think that's partly why I chose to go when I did. It was chilly that afternoon, even though most of the snow had melted. Nothing had turned green yet, but the geese were flying and the crows were haunting the trees and outbuildings.

By the time I got to the farm, my hands were cold, but I was glowing inside from the ride. I leaned my bike on the wire fence that closed off the house from the farmyard. It felt strange, standing there alone on the steps and knocking on the door, half hoping that Mrs. MacLaren wouldn't answer, and half hoping she would, because I wanted to be there without Ernie.

"Hello, Percy," she said as she opened the door. "This is a surprise."

Mrs. MacLaren was one of the few people who called me by my real name, except for my mother, who only called me Percy when she was about to ream me out for something.

I knew something was different as I walked into the kitchen. It was as spotless as ever, but I could see no evidence of baking or even anything on the stove for dinner that night. Then I remembered about Saturdays. Mrs. MacLaren asked me about school, and asked about Ernie and what he was doing, and then she set a plastic container full of cookies on the table.

"Help yourself," she said. "I'm sorry they're not fresh, but I have to go into town this afternoon and I haven't done any baking today."

I looked at her and knew that whatever was taking Mrs. MacLaren into town must be more than just shopping. She was dressed up more than I'd ever seen.

"I'm starting a new job today, Percy," she said brightly, "so I'll have to be off soon, but Mr. MacLaren's out in the barn. I think he's working on the starter for the tractor. Perhaps you could go and give him a hand. I'm sure he wouldn't mind the help."

I was certain Mr. MacLaren wasn't going to be grateful for any help. Something else didn't ring true about her words or her tone, but I didn't understand. Whatever was going on, I knew she was trying to get rid of me, and I felt strange there on my own, without Ernie to keep the talk going in a way that I couldn't, or to make Mrs. MacLaren laugh in a way that I wasn't able. I didn't argue, but grabbed some of the cookies from the container and left as quickly as possible.

Out in the barn, Mr. MacLaren was peering into the open hood of the tractor. He just looked at me as I walked in, and I felt I had to say something before he sent me packing.

"Mrs. MacLaren thought you could use my help." It sounded stupid, even to me, but I was desperate to say something. He grunted and looked over at the starter spread out on the workbench.

So I helped. I didn't do much except hand him tools, or hold one end of the starter while he cleaned it. I knew something about engines from watching my dad at the garage, so if I wasn't much help, I knew I wasn't entirely in the way.

He worked silently and methodically, hardly speaking, save for when he asked me for a tool. I found myself watching his hands as he worked. I had already noticed those hands—narrow and fine-boned, and so unlike my father's broad fingers and thick, hardened palms. Now and again I would look up at his face. His right side was toward me, and I only occasionally saw the left, with its scarred, unflinching skin and staring eye. The right side of his face was smooth as well, but full of fine lines around eye and mouth that belied the perpetual expressionlessness of his face.

We got the starter back into the tractor, and Mr. MacLaren stood by the workbench cleaning his hands with a rag. The afternoon was getting late.

I felt elated, partly because I knew that I had been able to help in a way that Ernie never could. Ernie knew nothing about engines or cars—or tools, for that matter—and I had been helpful, feeling an odd kinship with this man whom I hardly knew.

"Why do you keep looking at me?"

The question cut into my thoughts, raking across my awareness like metal across concrete. He was staring at me—glaring, actually, full-faced and pissed off. I was stunned. I had crossed some unforgivable line, and I just stood there not knowing what I had done or what to say.

"If you just came here to goddamn well stare, then you can get the hell out!"

I was still staring back at him, unable to say anything. It was like receiving an unexpected blow. I began backing away from him. His anger made me want to run, and I felt sick and ashamed, still not knowing what I had done.

He opened his mouth to say something else, but I was out the barn door and running across the yard. I yanked my bike away from the fence and pedaled as hard as I could down the drive and onto the road, my legs feeling weird and shaky, just as they did in dreams when I couldn't escape something that was going to kill me or eat me. I rode and rode.

Back in town, I didn't go home—I went to the garage. I'm not sure why. My father was usually the last person I went to when I was upset. The bay doors were open, and I leaned my bike against the wall and went inside. My dad's legs were stuck out from beneath an old Buick, and I could hear him breathing from beneath the car, his legs twitching as he struggled with whatever he was doing.

"Toby?" I heard him say.

"Yeah," I said, my voice a dry croak. I sat down on an old transmission set on cinder blocks and began to cry. I hated crying, but I couldn't help it. I tried not to make any noise, only sniffing hard against the tears and the thing that was burning a hole in my chest.

And suddenly there was my father, looking red-faced and grimy, wiping the sweat off his face with an old rag.

"Toby?" he said again, looking at me strangely. And then I really did cry, great gasping sobs that tore at my stomach. My father stared and reached out one hand to me, stopping midway to look down at the grease and dirt blackening his palm and fingers, before dropping it back to his side.

"Toby, what is it?"

But I only shook my head.

After my father cleaned his hands and set the garage in order, we went home. I loaded my bike onto the back of the truck and climbed into the cab. My father said nothing to me on the way home, and I simply sat there in ashamed silence.

After supper, during which I pushed the food around on my plate, I disappeared into the basement. My mother didn't seem to notice my silence, and for once didn't get after me about finishing my dinner.

I was shoving toys around in an old box when my mother came down the stairs. She sat on the edge of the old steamer trunk and looked at me. "Mrs. MacLaren called a few minutes ago." It was a statement, and she waited for me to respond.

I didn't say anything, but picked up the receiver from an old plastic telephone.

"Did something happen when you went to the MacLaren place this afternoon?"

I shrugged, but still said nothing.

My mother sat in silence for a long time, and then she sighed. "Mr. MacLaren was angry about something…I think, Percy," she said after a minute, "that you shouldn't go out there anymore."

I nodded my head, lightly tapping the plastic phone against the edge of the box.

She sighed again. "It's late. You should get ready for bed."

I nodded and slid away from her and up the stairs. My bike was still in the box of my father's truck, so I went outside to put it away. He always left the truck in the drive and parked the car in the garage.

I walked across the yard and into the alley, where my dad parked the truck. It was a cloudless night, and the stars burned hard and clear in a black sky. The newly formed ice cracked and popped underfoot, and I felt a remoteness that was reflected back to me from the black sky. I felt hollow and far away inside myself, just as I sometimes remembered feeling upon waking up Christmas morning. But this hollowness seemed like a permanent thing, and there seemed to be nowhere for me to turn. After putting my bike away in the garage, I walked slowly back toward the house. I hung back in the darkness, looking at the house with the lights from the kitchen cast down onto the sidewalk. Its walls were solid and dark, able to keep things out, but they offered no sanctuary for me. I felt my own walls falling into place, walls that were meant as much to keep things out as they were to keep things in. I walked slowly across the grass, still winter brown and frozen in patches where meltwater had gathered. I listened to the popping of the ice as I made my way across the yard, and by the time I came back into the light, the memory of that day was fading into the night, dissipating into a day of early spring, becoming a memory on the air, easily forgettable but forever burned into my heart.

MY BROTHER'S KEEPER

Robert sat at the kitchen table, trying not to think about the day. He wished like hell that he was anywhere else. Outside, the sky was a clear, pale blue. The morning sun slanted into the kitchen through the side windows and down over the roof of the house into the empty garden, glancing off the white stucco of the garage. He had helped build that garage. It had been one of his father's last projects before he'd died sixteen—no, seventeen—years ago. But the garden had always been his mother's. For as long as he could remember, starting on the May long weekend, she had been out there every day, planting, transplanting, stringing beans on poles, propping up her tomatoes, and weeding—always goddamn weeding. And now she was dead, too, and her garden was just an empty stretch of ground that he could hardly stand to look at, only made worse by the fact he was in the house doing the very thing his mother had never wanted.

Robert turned from the window as the coffee began to boil and sputter. He reached over and turned down the gas so the coffee perked slowly. He would be glad when this day was over. All he wanted was to be done with this house, to get Tom into the home, and get back to town.

It hadn't seemed like a week; it seemed like a year. The funny thing was, it hadn't been the cancer that killed her, after all. Ten months and two operations later, she hadn't seemed any closer to dying than when they had first found the cancer. And then there had been the call. He had been half expecting a call for months. She had grown thinner since Christmas, but she still tried to do everything she had always done before getting sick. When the snow began to melt, he thought for sure she would want to be outside doing something stupid like taking off the storm windows or cleaning the eaves. She would fall and break her hip, and he would have to drive into the city to see her in the hospital and stand beside her bed, guilty as hell, while she looked at him in that way she had, the look she gave him when he was twelve and she caught him smoking in the garage.

He had expected the call to come from the police, even a neighbour. But it had been Tom who called: Tom—his blind brother, sheltered from everything his whole life—as cool as anything, telling him that their mother had been pronounced dead on arrival at the hospital after suffering a massive stroke. Robert had felt as though someone had kicked him in the stomach. After he got his breath, his first thought had been, What the fuck was she doing dying of a stroke when she was supposed to be dying of cancer?

Robert glanced back at the pot to check the coffee. Sarah was still downstairs packing, and from the bedroom he could hear Tom listening to one of his books. Robert glared at the softly perking coffee.

Jesus!

He didn't know why Tom had to play his books so loud. He wanted to go tell him to turn it down, and at the same time he felt a creeping sense of guilt for even wanting to.

Lying in bed the night before, he had made a crack about Tom listening to that goddamn tape player half the night again. Sarah had gone still beside him. "Rob," she'd said, her voice level in the darkness. "Tom has very little. Don't begrudge him his books. And anyway," she added, a different note entering her voice as she rolled onto her side, "after tomorrow you won't have to worry about it."

"But the case worker said…"

"I know what the case worker said." Sarah's voice was flat in the darkness. "He can't look after himself. He either lives with us or he goes into a home."

"He's not an idiot, for Christ's sake." Was he defending his brother?

"Of course he's not an idiot. But he can't look after himself. My god! Your mother wouldn't even send him to school."

So that had been that, and Robert had been awake half the night anyway, his mind filling up with all the things he was trying not to think about, while Sarah softly slept beside him.

Putting Tom into the home had been the only real solution. What to do with him once their mother was dead had not really been a question, at least not for Robert. For Sarah, it was different. He knew, had known for a long time, that Sarah would quit her job in a heartbeat—quit her job to take in a forty-two-year-old blind man who couldn't look after himself, and who spent his days listening to books and drinking coffee.

Maybe it was a maternal thing. That was probably it. Having kids was something they had talked about—just not something they had done. Sarah was only thirty. But Tom was a full-time job, and Robert could not imagine a future with Tommy as an endless, needy presence.

Robert was at the sink rinsing out the three remaining coffee mugs when Tom made his way into the room. He moved slowly, his hands slightly extended, those large, soft, pink hands with fingers that seemed to test the air before him.

"Coffee, Tom?"

Tom settled himself in his chair at the end of the table. "Thank you, Robby," he said.

Robert rolled his eyes and stepped back to the stove for the pot. Tom was the only person in the bloody world who still called him Robby. Robert filled the mugs at the counter, added cream to Sarah's, two teaspoons of sugar instead of three to Tom's, and brought them to the table.

"Sarah," he called. "Coffee."

"All right," came the muffled voice. "Be right there."

Robert set Tom's coffee down in front of him, and the big hands came up to encircle the cup. Robert looked at Tom for a moment and then away. He felt that same tiny rush of guilt whenever he looked at his brother. It was unfair, somehow—this looking—like watching someone from behind one-way glass.

Looking at Tom, really looking, had always been like seeing a distorted and distended image of himself. Years ago, whenever he had been out somewhere with Tom, which lately hadn't been very often, someone would say something about the resemblance between them. Whoever the hell they were would look at Tom, look at Robert, and say, always with an edge of incredulity: "Are you two twins?"

Tom looked older than Robert now, but that was only because of his thinning hair and stooped shoulders. Robert had all his hair, but he looked like hell, twenty years behind a desk working for weeklies, with the ass to show for it.

What unnerved Robert the most was to see his own expressions mirrored in his brother's face. Tom's emotions were plain to see, one expression chasing another across his soft, pale features. But Tom angry or upset was when Robert saw himself most clearly, and seeing himself like that always gave him a sickening feeling, as though he were being sucked out through the top of his head.

"The sun feels nice this morning," said Tom.

"Yeah," said Robert, feeling caught out.

God, Tom wasn't stupid, for Christ's sake. Not unaware. Sharp as a tack, really, in a funny sort of way. He read a lot, and when he wasn't reading, he listened to the radio—CBC mostly.

It had always surprised Robert just how much Tom knew about what was going on in the world, considering he hardly ever left the house. Looking at Tom across the table again, Robert felt that uneasy mix of loyalty and embarrassment that had been with him ever since they had been kids. He wished he could say something to Tom—anything, especially today—but he couldn't think of a thing.

Sarah came clattering up the stairs and into the kitchen. "Morning, Thomas," she said. Her face was pink and her eyes bright as she plunked herself down at the window end of the old table. "Better watch that coffee. Rob made it."

Tom laughed his high-pitched laugh.

Robert gave her a sour look.

"Well, Thomas," she said, "it's a beautifully bright morning."

Tom nodded as he slurped his coffee.

Robert groaned inwardly. Why the hell did she have to talk like that? It was like sharing the breakfast table with Mary fucking Poppins.

Sarah gave him a stony stare.

"Did you sleep any better last night, Thomas?"

"Yes, thank you," said Tom. His voice had a slight lisp.

Robert suddenly wanted a smoke.

"I know this is going to be a difficult day for you, and I know this has all been very sudden, but I think once you settle in at the home, you'll find it to be a good place after all. And we'll come and see you on the weekends. I'll come for sure, but I may have to drag your brother away from his desk." She paused for breath and gave Robert a look. "You will have your own room," she continued, looking back at Tom. "And you can read to your heart's content."

Tom nodded his head. "Mama would have it so."

Mama!

Fuck! Why did he have to call her that?

Robert stood. "I'll put your things in the car, Tom."

Robert lugged the heavy suitcase out the front door and dropped it into the trunk with a thud. He fumbled his pack from a pocket and lit a cigarette. The morning was cool and still. Here, the sun shone directly down into the front yard, lighting the two stunted maples and the front of the house with a soft glow. From somewhere not far away he could hear the insistent cawing of a crow. With an odd sense of shock, he realized it was spring. He hadn't really thought about it until just this moment. It seemed only a couple of weeks ago there had still been snow on the ground. There probably had been, but it bothered him that he couldn't remember. It was like that, though: one day it was winter, and then suddenly it would be spring. But this year he couldn't remember when the thaw had started. As he struggled to remember past the drive into the city and Tom's phone call, he suddenly thought of spring when he was eight or nine, of wearing great gum boots, three sizes too large, of melting snow and muddy water, and of wading through the mud hole that was the Richardsons' backyard, watching the brown water rise slowly to his boot tops. He looked again at the house. The tangled remains of the Manitoba maples cut across the half-formed memory.

He would never know why in the hell his mother had not cut down those goddamn trees. Five years ago a limb had come down on the front steps during a storm. She had a neighbour prune the trees back to the trunks, leaving two twenty-foot stumps topped by a tangle of branches. They stood there for all the world like inverted exclamation marks, as oddball as everything else about the place. Here lives an old woman with her blind son, and isn't she a goddamn saint for keeping him at home and looking after him for all these years. But it didn't matter anymore. It didn't matter a goddamn, because she was dead, and Tom was going into the home, and after today the house would be sold and nobody would care one way or the other.

It took a long time for the three of them to get out the door. Tom had to sip his way through exactly two and a half cups of coffee and munch his way through two pieces of toast, while he talked to Sarah about some book Robert had never heard of. And then finally they were out the door and on their way.

Robert hunched over the wheel as he drove. He took the freeway across the river, not because it was the quickest way to the home but because he liked to have a stretch of road in front of him. Sarah chatted away to Tom, who sat quietly, hands folded, in the backseat.

At the home, Robert grimly followed Sarah and Tom with the suitcase. Sarah carried Tom's talking-book machine, while Tom clutched her arm and gripped his white cane in the other hand. Robert didn't look at Tom. He kept his eyes focused on the back of Sarah's legs—good legs, firm and well muscled from years of running.

An efficient-looking woman about fifty wearing a nurse's uniform met them just inside the main doors. She barely glanced at Robert, greeting Sarah and shaking Tom firmly by the hand. She led the way down a corridor, Tom still moving at his cautious gait and clutching at Sarah's elbow, while Robert followed, his own breath sounding loud in the quiet. The place reminded Robert of a hospital; it didn't quite have the hospital smell, but it had the same feel.

Around a corner, through a door, and Robert could finally put down the suitcase. It was a small room: a bed, a bureau, a black vinyl chair with wooden arms, an end table beside the chair, and that was all. The windows were high and wide, and sunlight filled the little room.

Robert squinted as he tried to get his breath. He stood, hands hanging at his sides, watching Sarah bustle about the room and exclaiming over this and that, her voice sounding loud and unnatural. The whole time Sarah was talking, Tom explored the room bit by bit, touching the bed, running his hands over the bureau, the windowsill, and the drapes. He said nothing, moving methodically from one thing to another. He could have been alone in the room for all he paid attention to Sarah's chatter.

"Robert," said Sarah, still in that odd voice. "Put Thomas's suitcase on the bed and we'll get it unpacked."

Robert looked at her sourly. She was bloody well going to organize the room before they left.

He wrestled the suitcase onto the bed, and was suddenly and painfully aware of his bladder. This place made him twitchy as hell. His skin was clammy and he could feel the sweat beginning to run down his sides. He tried to catch the matron's eye.

"Is there a—uh—gent's?" he asked huskily.

She barely gave him a glance, jabbing a finger toward the door. "Down the hall and past the main doors."

Robert hurried down the hall. A smoke—that's what he really wanted. He got an inquiring look from a white uniform as he passed the common area opposite the main doors. He took another hall until he finally found the door marked Gentlemen and pushed his way inside. He stood there, sweat cooling over his back and arms, the relief of the piss giving him the chance to get his head together.

Back in the room, Tom was sitting in the armchair, and Sarah was still putting his things away, rattling hangers in the closet and opening and closing the bureau drawers.

No sign of the matron. What a fucking dragon.

Once everything was put away, Sarah knelt down before Tom. "We're going to have to go now, Thomas," she said gently. "I've got to catch the eleven o'clock back to town, and Rob has to finish up at the house, but we'll come and see you in a few days. Rob is in town until tonight, so he'll stop in again before he heads back." She gave Robert a pointed look.

Robert came forward. He grasped Tom's hand; it was moist and weak. "You'll be fine here, Tom," he said. "They'll look after you. It seems like a good place. I'll see you tonight, just to check in on you, you know. Come see you before I head back."

Sarah didn't look at him. Tom nodded his head. "Tonight," he said.

Robert couldn't tell what was going on inside Tom's head; his face was unreadable. He just sat there and kept nodding his head, one forefinger tracing patterns on the arm of the chair.

Sarah said nothing on the drive to the bus depot; she never even looked at him. Robert was uneasy, glancing at her from time to time, wondering what she was thinking. He parked the car and followed Sarah into the depot. "I'll see you tonight," he said as she took her place in line. "Probably late."

She nodded. "You will stop and see him." It was a statement, not a question. Her face was taught in the weird light of the depot.

"I'll stop," said Robert. And then he left her in the line, hurrying back to the car.

Getting the last of the things out of the house took longer than Robert wanted. He had to stop at the Realtor's to sign more papers, and then hang about until school was out so he could get some help from a neighbour kid—a sullen little prick in a baseball cap—to clear out the beds, the table and chairs, and the last of the boxes.

With the U-Haul loaded and the house locked, Robert pulled away from the house with a sense of relief. He didn't look back.

He stopped for a burger and fries, and by the time he was on his way again, it was after eight o'clock. All he wanted was to get home, but he had to stop in and see Tom before heading out of the city. He took the freeway again. It was still light, and the sky was full of evening. Below the bridge the river ran darkly, and to his right the sun had set behind downtown, the dark buildings standing out against the sky. It would be good to get on the highway. He liked driving at night.

Robert could have sworn that the matron was waiting for him at the front when he walked in. There she stood, and this time Robert had all her scathing attention. Her look was hard, but she didn't have to say anything. He could hear the sound from all the way down the corridor. He felt a hot rush, as something like a hand seemed to clamp itself around his chest. He hurried down the hall toward Tom's room.

Tom sat in the armchair, as if he hadn't moved the entire time Robert had been gone. But he was crying. No, fuck, he was wailing. His hands clutched at his knees and his face tilted slightly upward, the tears rolling down his cheeks and running off his jaw. But it was the sound that caused the prickle at the base of Robert's spine. Tom was keening, howling like a wounded animal, the sound interrupted only by Tom's need to take a breath. Robert was reminded of a dog his father had run over one summer morning a block from the house: a screech of brakes, a sickening bump, and his father swearing. Robert had stared transfixed at the dog as it cried and writhed in pain, its back broken, while his father ran to call the SPCA.

Robert stepped forward. "Tom! For Christ's sake, Tom!" He had seen Tom upset; he had seen Tom cry. But Jesus.

"Tommy!"

But there was no stopping him. His back arched with every breathy, wet sob, and the noise seemed to go on and on. Robert turned to look at the matron. She had followed him into the room, but now just stood there, her eyes calm and accusing. He looked back at Tom. What the hell was he supposed to do? The noise was making him crazy; he wanted it to stop. He wanted Tom to stop this—whatever the hell it was.

Robert went onto his knees in front of Tom, and he caught at one of the clutching hands. It gripped Robert's hand so tightly that he winced.

"Robby," said Tom, between one sob and the next.

Robert waited.

"Robby," came the choking voice again.

"Tommy! Calm down, will you," said Robert. "What the hell is this about?" He wanted to shake Tom, to yell at him, all the while half-afraid of this insane show of blubbering emotion.

The matron stepped up beside the armchair and firmly placed a kidney-shaped washbasin and facecloth on the end table. Robert looked at her and then at the washbasin. She turned and left the room without a word. Robert pulled his hand away from the quivering, sweaty clutch. "Here," he said. "Here." Tom's face was a smear of tears and snot.

Robert squeezed out the facecloth and clumsily placed it in Tom's hand. He found that his own hands were shaking as much as Tom's. "Now wipe your face, and tell me what this is all about."

Tom dragged the cloth over his face. "It's Mama, Robby," he said finally. "She's gone, gone forever. I didn't think about it until this afternoon, not until after you and Sarah left."

Another sob caught at his throat. "I was just sitting here, and all I could think about was that Mama's dead. She's dead, and she's never coming back."

Christ!

"I just miss her, Robby. I didn't think about it much before, but being here, being in this place rather than at home, helped me to understand that I just miss her. I sat here this afternoon, and it was as if she had died a long time ago, and I'd been here for years."

Robert tried to think, tried to understand what Tom was saying. She was dead—sure, but it wasn't as though they hadn't known it was coming. Maybe not a stroke, but there had been the cancer. And it had happened quickly. Then there was the house to clear out, and getting Tom ready to move into the home. Robert hadn't thought about it—about her being dead—or maybe he hadn't wanted to. He wondered if what he felt was anything like Tom's blubbering grief, but he didn't think so. He didn't really feel much of anything. Relief, maybe. She was dead, and he didn't have to feel as though she were looking at him anymore.

Robert looked up into Tom's face, almost masklike with its grimace of pain. Robert felt less shaky now that Tom was talking, and in a funny way seeing him like this almost made it easier for Robert to talk to him—like when they were kids. Robert would drag Tom outside to play cowboys or something, and Tom, every time, would get hurt, and Robert would try to comfort him, until their mother would appear like the wrath of God to give Robert hell and pull Tom back into the house.

"Is that what it is, Tom?" he asked now, still trying to understand. "Are you sure it isn't this place? Do you want to leave here? Do you want to be somewhere else?"

Robert suddenly had a sense of what it would be like with Tom living in the house in Galahad, of what it would be like having him there all the time. But they weren't kids anymore, and this would be different. It would be like having his mother there, only worse because he would be doing what she had wanted him to do all his life: taking care of his blind brother. He wouldn't do that; he couldn't. And anyway, their mother was dead, and Tom was here now.

Tom's voice made Robert look back up at his brother's face. "No," Tom said, frowning slightly. "I should stay here. Mama didn't want me to be a burden to you."

"Burden! What the hell is that supposed to mean?" Robert had the craziest desire to laugh, and at the same time he felt as though he had just stepped up to the edge of a cliff. "Tommy, you're my brother, for Christ's sake."

"No." Tom had on his stubborn look. "Mama wanted me to be in a place where I would be looked after, and she didn't want you to be responsible for me."

"She said that?" Robert gripped the arm of the chair with one hand while still holding Tom's hand with the other. "When did she say that?"

"I'm not sure," said Tom, frowning again. "Around the time she first got sick. She said it would be better for me and for you if I came to a place like this, the sort of place where I could get lots of help. I know I can't look after myself."

Robert was looking at his brother as though he had never seen him before. His face was still tear-streaked and blotchy from crying, but there was something in Tom's voice that made Robert stare. He had never heard Tom talking like this, so matter-of-factly, with no excuses for the way things were or had always been.

"It's not as though I never wanted to do things for myself, you know," said Tom, with a small sort of dignity. "Mama just seemed so happy doing things for me that I couldn't disappoint her."

Disappoint her.

Fuck.

It was too strange hearing Tom talk like this, too unlike the way Robert thought things were, or always had been—the story Robert had lived by all his life unraveling before him.

"But I would like it if you came to visit," Tom continued. "Sarah, too, but just you sometimes."

"Of course, Tommy. I'll come." Robert tried to give the words some force, but they didn't sound very convincing, even to him.

Outside the home, the cool evening was gathering toward night. Robert walked slowly, trying to understand what had happened. He had stayed with Tom awhile longer, not really wanting to stay but hating to leave. After Tom had said his piece, he seemed okay; it was Robert who had trouble getting out the door. Walking out had been hard, as though he was never going to see Tom again, or as though he were cutting himself off from something.

Robert stopped by the fender of the car to light a cigarette. He looked up. The sky was an inky blue darkening to black.

He would visit Tom, just as he promised. But it wouldn't be the same, somehow. He knew that, without really knowing how it would be different. And he had an odd sense of forgetting something, as if he had left something behind somewhere, whether in the house on Eighty-Eighth Street or with Tom in the home he didn't know. It made him anxious just thinking about it. He couldn't put a name to it, anyway; he only knew it by its absence, and all that was left was the space where it had been. Standing there by the fender of the car, with stars beginning to prick the sky and the light from the streetlamps pooling on the road, Robert had a vaguely terrifying sense of what it would be like to live with that space now that he knew it was there, and he suddenly felt afraid of what his life would be like from now on.

CHINA DOLLS

"You don't look like my daughter," said Rose, watching the woman who crouched beside her chair. "She moved out of the house a long time ago." Something was familiar about the middle-aged woman with the ashen-red hair, but Rose could not remember. The woman couldn't be her daughter; she was too old, for one thing. Stacey had no gray in her hair, and she certainly didn't wear glasses.

The middle-aged woman settled back on her heels. She had one hand on the arm of the chair and the other on Rose's hand. It was a thin hand, delicate as bone china, blue veins running just beneath the parchment-thin skin.

"I'm Stacey, Mom."

"But Stacey lives in Montreal," said Rose. She watched the younger woman.

Rose's eyes were a pale, rinsed blue, set in a thinning face framed by equally thinning white hair. At the moment the eyes had a puzzled expression, but Stacey knew those eyes could quickly become hard as glacial ice, hard-edged with suspicion and accusation. It was at such times that Stacey found it exhausting to look after her mother.

Stacey shifted her weight slightly. "Do you want your tea, Mom?"

Rose didn't seem to hear. "Stacey went to Montreal in the spring," she said. "She was going there to the university. I think she was interested in a boy, but I don't remember his name. He was going to the university as well. I told her it was a good idea to go to university. Marriage is good, but a young woman needs an education, and even an arts degree is an education of sorts—not like nursing or teaching, of course.

"My sister Fran was a teacher. She was a good girl—the oldest of us MacIntyre girls. She went to Normal School in Edmonton. Had her first teaching job at eighteen years old—a one-room school—outside Fort Macleod, I think."

As Rose spoke, her eyes grew distant, recounting the details of the past. She stopped, her eyes growing present and hard as she looked at Stacey. "And don't call me mom. You're somebody's daughter, but you're not mine." The truth of that statement was Rose's present, the reality that was hers as she stared down at the woman beside her.

Stacey felt the curl of something ugly low in her belly. Sometimes she couldn't help but believe the things Rose said. It was crazy—of course. Her mother's malleable sense of past and present sometimes infected her own. But Rose was sick; she couldn't help it.

Sometimes Stacey really didn't believe she was Rose's daughter. She was an impostor, a changeling child who had taken the place of the real Stacey. Stacey's past belonged to someone else, and this Stacey—this middle-aged, worn-out Stacey, who spent most days in sweats and old T-shirts—had stepped in to look after Rose as the older woman's mind slowly and inexorably self-destructed.

And it was slow—agonizingly slow. Stacey had watched as Rose lost bits of her present, sections flaking away here and there like shingles being blown off a roof. The bare patches grew larger and larger until whole swaths of the present were gone, and Rose's atrophying brain substituted older memories to fill the gaps, or simply made things up to compensate for what was missing.

"I'll get your tea, Rose."

Rose's eyes softened—ever so slightly. "Yes," she said, synaptic gears sliding and seeking purchase. "I would like some tea—in my old country cup, mind."

Stacey heaved herself to her feet, feeling the ache in her legs and lower back. She glanced at the clock on the mantel—almost two. The twins would be home from school in an hour. They would seek her attention, demand to tell her about their day. She would gather them close, stroke their braided hair, inhaling the smell of their girl bodies. Steph would be home later, whenever later was. Steph, her sixteen-year-old, in her spaghetti straps and crotch-crawler jeans, who looked at Stacey alternately with pity and contempt. Either one made Stacey itch to slap her smug face.

Stacey made the tea in the kitchen, watching out the window at the November rain. The cedars that stood near the house were darkly wet in the half-light of the afternoon, while the dogwood crouched like a shadow at the back of the yard.

What had happened to her life?

She might as well be someone else. The life she'd had once upon a time was gone. She went from days of running errands, walks on the beach, operating a small photography business, and coaching the twins' baseball team to this—her life reduced to the house and yard, watching the painful progression of the clock—day after bloody day—and having conversations with someone who no longer recognized her and who had lost all sense of past and present.

Before her mother began to forget things, before Rose moved into the house, Stacey's time had been her own. She had organized it, arranged it, and directed it like a maestro; now, as months had crept into years, she bartered for it—every scrap, every minute, and every chance she wanted alone. She was reminded of the early years with the twins while they still lived on Weiler, when she would lock herself in the bathroom with a magazine, trying to grab five minutes for herself until one of the twins would come tapping on the door.

She poured the tea into a cheap, imitation china cup. The cup had come from Zellers—or maybe it had been the Kmart on Shelbourne. Four identical cups were lined up in the cupboard. She had already broken two.

She carried the tea into the living room. Rose sat, vaguely watching the television. Stacey set the tea on the end table, carefully positioning it within reach of her mother's hand.

"Are you ready for a snack, Rose?" Stacey assumed the brightly brittle voice she used more and more often these days. She hated the sound of that voice coming from her own head.

Rose glanced over. "A snack. All right. That would be nice. Maybe some of those chocolate biscuits."

Her mother meant cookies. Rose loved those cookies. She would ask for them sometimes, looking up with a hopeful, tremulous expression that reminded Stacey of the twins—an expression that also held the disappointment of denial.

Stacey went to get the cookies.

Rose was staring at her cup when Stacey returned to the living room. She looked up at the younger woman.

"This cup reminds me of the china dolls I used to have." Rose frowned. "I'm not sure where they are. Do you know, dear?"

"I don't think so," said Stacey. "What did they look like?"

"They were china dolls. You know. Little figurines. My mother bought them as a present to herself before she came to Toronto. That was before the war. Can you imagine—coming to Toronto on her own, all the way from Scotland? She was very brave, my mother was. It was in Toronto that she met her husband. She was a Campbell before she married Alexander MacIntyre. They were married just two months before he left for France and the war. The Great War, mind. Fran was born while Daddy was away. Mother kept those china dolls on the mantel. She said she would look at them to remind herself of where she came from."

"Really," Stacey said distractedly. She looked at the clock again, and then turned her attention to the television. It looked like an infomercial—something about a gadget for chopping vegetables.

"Except I don't know where they are. That's odd, isn't it?" Rose frowned again. "Maybe I gave them to Stacey...That's right. I gave them to Stacey. She's getting married soon. And about time, too. A young woman needs to be married."

Stacey looked at her mother. When Rose got hold of a memory, she worried it like a dog with a bone.

"She's a good girl, Stacey. An education was a good thing, of course, but that girl was built for having children. It's about time she settled down and started a family."

Rose was settling placidly into her memory. "It's a nice fellow she's marrying—Kurt or Kirk, or something like that."

"Carter," Stacey said laconically.

Rose didn't notice. "I told Stacey that I would give her those dolls as a wedding present. My mother gave them to me, you see, and I wanted to give them to my daughter. Three generations of MacIntyre women. We can't forget who we are. Those dolls remind us. We're strong women and free. Good marriage material but smart."

Rose's face had relaxed into a satisfied expression, and Stacey watched it. Her mother looked so thin, and somehow translucent, but still the same woman who had a place in Stacey's own mind and memories—at least for now.

It was sometimes hard for Stacey to remember her mother before the dementia. But this had been the woman who had recovered from a divorce in 1965: the woman who went on to raise two children, who managed to save enough money from her job as a pharmacist to send both to university, and who had planned to happily retire on her pension—perhaps to travel a little, but mostly to visit her grandchildren.

But that hadn't happened. Stacey had been in the habit of talking to her mother on the phone every few days. Her brother, Greg, never kept in touch—the useless shit.

At first, the lapses in memory were small. Rose always brushed them off with a laugh—just a sign of old age. But one morning, as Stacey sat sorting photographs at the dining room table, Rose called to say that she couldn't find the house.

"I drove around for an hour, but I can't seem to find it," she had said in a half whisper, the desolate terror in her mother's voice making Stacey's lower spine tingle. And in that moment, Stacey could feel the gears of her life grinding, and even as she talked quietly and calmly to her mother, desperately trying to think of what to do, she knew that nothing would be the same again.

Two months and a garage sale later, Rose had sold the house in Edmonton, gotten rid of or given away most of her things, and she and Stacey and Carter were driving west along the Yellowhead, U-Haul in tow, making a beeline for the island and home.

Stacey looked at the clock again. The kids would be home soon, and she knew her tension would begin to subside with other people around to help reassert her life. But it would come back; it would come back with each day and its relentless attention to minutiae.

"I'll be right back, Rose." But her mother didn't notice. Rose was watching the TV, the cookie in her hand forgotten.

Stacey slipped out of the room and paced down the hall. She eased open the door that let her into the garage, crowded with boxes, family castoffs, and the last of her mother's furniture.

Bumping her way around the old Ping-Pong table, Stacey went to Carter's workbench. She reached up to a shelf to take down a delicate china doll. She gentled the thing in her hands for a moment, admiring the detail of the exquisitely drawn face and hair, the intricacies of the dress and its folds. And then she took up the hammer, set the exquisite thing carefully on the bench, and smashed it to fragments.

She had a box that she kept under the bench for the shards and crumbs of porcelain. She never told Carter what she did, and she had no idea what she'd do when the dolls ran out. She would have to find something else, something to help keep her in this present, her own present.

But it was only a matter of time before Rose would go to a home. Eventually, they would put Rose's name on a list. Stacey would get a call, and then she would pack up her mother and those few things that would help Rose to feel comfortable. And she and Carter would drive Rose to the home, where she would be looked after by strangers, while Stacey would be free to take back her life, to live in her own present, and visit her mother as she would a stranger.

MARTIE

Every year at Thanksgiving and Christmas my family has dinner at one of the aunts'. These are my mom's three sisters, all of whom make these amazing turkey dinners. My mom is the youngest in her family by something like twelve years, so she hardly ever gets to host the big family dinners. This year, Thanksgiving dinner is at Aunty Florence's, and Martie will be there.

Martie is ten years older than me, and I am in love with her. You probably think that it's just stupid for a scrawny fifteen-year-old to talk about being in love, but I've read enough to know that this is how it's supposed to feel. Martie is also my cousin, and you may find that even weirder. But before you make up your mind, I first have to tell you about her.

I know that real writers do the same thing by giving details of character and all that crap, but I'm not a real writer, and this isn't a real story, so you'll have to put up with me if you want to keep reading. Martie is taller than me by a couple of inches. She has shiny auburn hair that comes down to her shoulders. Her eyes are the family blue, large and clear, and her skin is this pale, translucent colour that has a kind of delicate look to it. She smells nice, too—not perfume or deodorant smell, but outside smell, fresh and clean. The only unusual thing about Martie, at least as far as my family is concerned, is that she touches everybody. She's always reaching out and touching the person she's talking to, which is how I got into trouble.

As for me, probably the only thing you need to know is that I read. I read a lot—all the time, in fact. I've read Hardy, Dickens, Twain, Austen, Hemingway, Conrad, and this weird writer named Lord Dunsany. At school, teachers are always impressed at how much I've read, but I don't talk about it too much because that's how you get punched. Without a doubt, I have read more than most people my age, and I read more than most people in my family, except for Aunt Florence, who is a teacher. And not just literature, either. I've read most of the Bible, which is more than I can say for first-cousin Susan, a born-again Christian who can't get a passage of scripture right to save her life.

Oh, the other thing is that I've been seeing a therapist for more than a year now. I'm not really a freak, although sometimes I feel like one. In junior high, I got beaten up a lot. Weird stuff started happening to me. I wet the bed a bunch of times—that was embarrassing. The worst was one evening in the department store. My mom left me in the menswear section to go and pay for something, and I started getting this buzzing sensation in my head. Pretty soon my heart was pounding and I couldn't breathe. I thought I was going to die, right there by the wall of men's pants. I don't remember very well, but I must have crawled under the rack. That's where they found me half an hour later, curled up against the wall under those pants.

My parents were worried. They sent me to this therapist at the beginning of grade nine, and I'm still seeing her. Things are better now. I started high school this fall, and I even have a friend, Tony, who is a geek, like me. We both read, but he's more into fantasy.

But that's enough of that. I don't suppose you're impressed, and you still probably think it's weird that I'm in love with my cousin, but I don't care. It's not going-out kind of love or anything like that. It's book love, not the groping sort of thing my two idiot older brothers do with their girlfriends whenever my parents are out, which, by the way, I can hear from upstairs while I'm watching TV.

I've had a crush on Martie since I was probably eight, but I've only been in love with her since last Christmas. A bunch of us were down in Calgary for Christmas dinner—again, one of the aunts.

My family and I got to Calgary around lunchtime, and Uncle Don, who always looks like somebody just woke him up from a nap, came to the door and ushered us in with the whole Merry Christmas routine. He even asked me if Santa was good to me, which got a smirk from my sister, who is, by the way, nineteen, in university, and stuck up. Aunty Nell was at the kitchen counter peeling about a million potatoes, and the house was full of the smell of roasting turkey. Aunty Nell told us to help ourselves to a tray of sandwiches in the fridge, and then told me, my dad, and my uncle Don to get lost while the women got dinner ready. I overheard my aunt telling my mom that they had a count of twenty for dinner, but most important was that Martie would be there. She is the only one of my relatives who takes me seriously. We always talk about books, and she always listens to whatever I have to say.

You need to remember that last Christmas I only had a crush on Martie, but I was excited at the thought of seeing her—excited in that nervous sort of way. It was Christmas, too, and Martie always dresses up for family dinners, and she always looks really nice. I dress up, too—usually my blazer and a bow tie.

I have to tell you something else about Martie that will help explain what happened. Martie is…ample. I read that in a book by Thomas Hardy. She has a small waist, which makes her look even bustier. This amplitude is a trait of all the Ferrier women, stuck-up Natalie included, which I hadn't really noticed until I started keeping track.

Relatives were beginning to arrive about halfway through the afternoon, and I took up a vantage point on a stool at one end of the food table. I had a view of the length of the living room in front of me and the kitchen to my right, and I kept an eye out for Martie as the house began to fill up with people. I was balancing a paper plate on one knee, holding a glass of punch in the other hand while trying to get a cheese and cracker sandwich into my mouth when Martie appeared out of nowhere. I couldn't believe it. My mouth crammed with cheese and cracker, I looked up to see her standing beside me, looking amazing in a black skirt and this filmy top.

She didn't wait. "Nick," she cried. "Merry Christmas." Leaning down, she hugged me head and shoulders so that the right side of my face landed right between those two round boobs. My glasses were knocked to one side, and for one dizzying second I was aware of slippery material, her clean smell, and my mouth, still crammed with cheese and cracker, momentarily flattened against the curve of one breast. And then she let me go.

By this time, I was coughing and trying to wash down the mess in my mouth with punch. I couldn't see anything because of my glasses, but also because my eyes were watering from humiliation and trying not to choke.

"I'm sorry, Nick," she said from somewhere above my head. I felt the paper plate leave my hand and a paper napkin take its place. "Here," she said, "and drink something before you choke to death."

I drank some punch and wiped my eyes with the napkin before straightening my glasses. There she was, smiling down at me, and I felt something happen inside my chest that I didn't understand.

It took me a while, but I finally figured out that I was in love with her. I had to read a lot in order to understand what happened, but once I did I spent time trying to imagine what I would say to her the next time I saw her. I thought about other stuff, too, but I'm not going to tell you about that.

Back to Thanksgiving. The drive out to Aunty Florence's was fairly short. They live in this little town called Galahad, where they moved after Uncle Don retired from farming. It sits there alongside the highway as though somebody had chucked it out of a moving truck. The idiot brothers weren't there and the ride out was quiet. Sister Natalie was reading a magazine, and for once I didn't feel like giving her a hard time.

We arrived at the house that stood at the end of this crescent thing in the newer part of town, and I could see there were at least twelve cars parked out front. Inside, the house was noisy and full of smells. Every one of my fifteen first cousins seemed to be there, from those dorky kids who live out on Aunty Florence and Uncle Don's old place to the ones about Natalie's age. No one was my age, which always made me feel like a bit of a freak.

But this time I didn't care. I made my way through the heat and clatter and chatter of the kitchen and into the living room. The husbands of the four sisters were seated around the punch bowl. They all looked as though they already had a good start on the punch, except for my dad. He doesn't drink anymore.

So where was Martie?

I found her in the rumpus room downstairs. A bunch of kids were playing pool, and others were playing darts or watching TV. Martie was sitting on one of the couches talking with Rob, this professor guy who is married to second cousin Betsy. There he sat, spiffed up in his professor's blazer with the leather patches on the elbows. I couldn't read the expression on Martie's face. She had her hands folded in her lap as he leaned in toward her with whatever he was saying.

I gave up trying to get her attention and wandered back upstairs. It felt strange seeing her like that. I wanted to talk to her, but how could I, with *Mr. Hello I'm an Important College Man* breathing all over her?

Aunty Florence caught me in a hug when I came back to the kitchen, and my mom shot me a warning glance as I snatched a bit of turkey from one of the platters on the counter.

"Let him be, Hope," said Aunty Florence. "He's a growing boy."

My mom ignored the comment and told me to get lost. My mom gets tense at these dinners. She hates her name, for one thing. She goes by her middle name, which is Pat—short for Patricia—but her sisters insist on calling her Hope.

I went into the living room to find the kids' punch bowl. My uncles were all well on their way with theirs, while my dad sat with them, balancing a cup of coffee on his knee. They were talking politics—something about Trudeau and the goddamn federal government—which meant that they were starting to get drunk.

I found the kids' punch and filled a plastic cup. I stared out the front window, which gave the long view of that nothing street, houses to either side staring across at one another with nothing to say. It was growing dusk. I didn't know why I felt the way I did, whatever that was. Maybe it was just seeing Martie with that college goof. I drank my punch and started eating from the snack table.

Supper happened in the living and dining rooms. Relatives were strewn about on couches and chairs, and there were two extra tables set up for those who didn't want to eat from a plate in their lap. I squeezed myself into the corner of a couch and picked at my dinner. Martie was sitting at the other end of the room on a straight-backed chair. My aunty Florence makes about the best turkey dinner going, but I had lost my appetite. I didn't look at Martie, and I didn't even try to listen to the conversations around me.

After dinner, I was standing in the kitchen, backed up against the wall out of the way. I had done my part by going around with a green garbage bag to collect used paper plates and cups. My mom gets really mad if I don't do something to help out at these dinners. I was standing and watching the chaos of cleanup when I looked to my right down the hallway. Martie was standing there at the end of the hall, half turned away from me. Right beside her was Mr. College Professor and I saw him suddenly reach out a hand and place it on her hip. Not on her waist, and not just on her hip bone. He had his hand on that fleshy part of a woman's hip, right above the back pocket if she's wearing jeans. I stared. And at that moment, Martie looked past him and saw me staring. I didn't wait; I fled.

I pounded down the stairs. No one was in the basement; they were all upstairs, waiting for pie and ice cream. It seemed empty and silent down there with all the noise coming from overhead.

I didn't know what to do or think. I walked over to the pool table and started chucking balls around. I chucked them harder and harder so they cracked together and sometimes thunked into a pocket. I went around and picked balls out of pockets and put them back in motion. Soon I had that whole table cracking and bouncing. My mom would have killed me if she saw what I was doing, but I didn't care.

"Nick."

I stopped dead and looked around. Martie stood in the door to the rumpus room.

"What are you doing?"

I didn't answer, just looked back at her. Her face seemed paler than usual, save for two spots of colour to either side of her nose.

"Nick, I want to talk to you."

In the sudden silence, I stared back at her.

"Upstairs. It wasn't what you think."

I didn't want to listen. I tried to move past her. I just wanted to get away.

"Nick," she said again, but this time in this breathy sort of voice that made me look up. She was still looking at me, and I stared back, unable to read the expression there. But right then she reached up her hands toward my shoulders.

I guess I blurted something, but I don't remember. Next thing I knew I was running down the hall bawling my face off. I ran up the stairs and straight out the door. I didn't stop at the end of the yard but headed right out to the street. I ran and ran.

I didn't stop until I was away from the houses and onto a wider street with an open field in front of me. It was dark, but I couldn't see anything anyway because I was still crying. I pulled off my glasses and rubbed my face on the sleeve of my blazer. I felt like an idiot—humiliated and stupid.

It was quiet, except for the sound of my own breath. The field stretched away in front of me, and far off I could see the lights of cars passing on the highway. They made a faint tearing sound as they went by.

I knew I had to go back. It was freezing, for one thing, but I couldn't just yet. Craning my neck, I looked up to see about a million stars in a black arch of sky. Everything I had read, everything I had tried to understand from books, wasn't enough. And I laughed. It was one of those crying sort of laughs that make you sound a little crazy.

And for one giddy second, I felt like a character in a book. Not like one of those guys who figures it all out, but one of those who never gets it right. And with one more sniff and a shiver from the cold, I turned and headed back up the street to my aunt's.

SCAVENGERS

My family left Galahad the summer I turned thirteen. My dad sold the garage in town, we moved into the city, and I didn't go back for more than thirty years. When I do go back, driving out on an afternoon while both kids are in school, I see that very little has changed. There is a new subdivision south of the arena, and the town has a new hospital, but the curling rink is still there, and my dad's old garage doesn't look much different than it had when we left. Ed's feed shop is still there, too, looking small and abandoned, right at the end of the old hospital road that runs east out of town. The hospital road here meets the range road, and I get out of my car to follow the road on foot through fields of standing grain and open pastures, where I can see cattle stupidly chewing in the pale October sun.

Ed Jenkins owned that feed shop when I was a kid. He bought it from old man Seversen, who used the building as a creamery for as long as anyone in town could remember; by the time Ed bought it, the building had already been empty for ten years. Ed bought the building so he could sell horse feed, but he wasn't much better at running a business than he was at running a farm. Ed's business sense wasn't like many people's in Galahad. He was a failure as a farmer, and a lousy feed salesman, but he was a first-rate scavenger, and at least half a crook.

Ernie and I spent a lot of time together in the year before my father sold the garage. We were in the same class in grade seven, and Ernie's interests that year were limited to cars and sex. Cars were easy.

My father ran one of the two body shops in town, and sometimes after school Ernie would wheedle me into going to visit the garage where we would usually find my dad, red-faced and greased to the elbows, with his head in the open hood of somebody's Buick or Plymouth doing repairs. Ernie would peer over my dad's arm and ask questions. I would usually stand against the wall or sit on a tire and wait until my dad told us to get lost. He would always put up with us for a while, but eventually he would tell us that he was busy and that we should go and play or something.

Ernie was always reluctant to leave, but we never stuck around. "Play," said Ernie once as we left the body shop. He looked disgusted. "Who the hell does he think he is, anyway? We ain't kids."

I didn't respond to this or any of Ernie's tirades. I only ever felt a tightness in my chest that I would come to know as the debilitating anxiety of my adulthood.

Ernie's desire for detail in that year extended to sex as well as cars. We were both curious, but it wasn't as though either of us had ever done it, as Ernie used to say. We just talked about it. I knew people did it, and I knew cows did it, but somehow I couldn't reconcile the two.

"I have something for you," Ernie said one day after school, in that self-satisfied way he had when he knew about something I didn't.

It was late afternoon in the fall of grade seven, the air full of grain dust from the harvest, and the sunset burning the sky to a bloody orange. We were riding our bikes out of town, heading past Ed's feed shop and onto the range road.

"What is it?" I asked, pedaling along.

"You gotta keep your shirt on," said Ernie, grinning behind his glasses.

We rode about a mile until we came to old Alex Rimbey's place, who I knew was a cousin or something to Ernie's dad. We dumped our bikes in the drive and I looked around, feeling like an intruder. "Maybe we should tell somebody we're here," I said, following Ernie to one of the outbuildings.

"Nah. Alex won't care, and we're just going to have a look behind his barn."

I trailed after him, still feeling odd at coming onto the Rimbeys' property like this. Ernie led me around the corner of the barn to a fence that enclosed a small building like a granary. He looked around and, still grinning, put his finger to his lips and began to climb the fence.

We got over that wooden fence without too much trouble and dropped onto the bare earth on the other side. Ernie crooked his finger and led me toward what was once a door to the old granary. Getting close enough to peer around the corner, I saw perhaps the biggest boar I had ever seen in my life. The thing was immense. Its head and shoulders were screened by the frame of the door, but I could see the ridge of its back, bristling with black hair, and its massive haunch, as big as a cow's, perched on two ridiculously short back legs.

Ernie prodded me and pointed to the underbelly, where I saw something I didn't recognize at once for what they were—testicles, enormous fucking testicles the size of small grapefruits that swayed slightly as the bore shifted its weight. Maybe I moved; maybe I made a noise. I don't know. But suddenly the massive shape gave a jerk, and Ernie and I tore away from the door and back to the fence, my heart hammering and my brain screaming as I waited for the thing to come out of the granary and rip us to shreds with tusks that I hadn't seen but could imagine well enough. I clawed my way over the fence, my insides turning to water as we raced back to our bikes and tore out of the yard.

That was Fred, I later learned. I had been impressed by the size of his balls, but I never cared to repeat the visit. It was like that with Ernie: he was impressed by size, and he gave me graphic descriptions of Fred humping sows in that pen. I wanted to hear about it, but at the same time I didn't.

As the world of sex began to open up for me in that year, it became much more complicated than I had at first thought. It was much more than Fred and his grapefruit-size balls.

One Sunday morning, hurrying downstairs to the bathroom because of the urgent pressing of my bladder, I heard sounds as I passed my parents' bedroom. I stopped dead at the foot of the stairs and listened: a sucking breath from my father and a guttural sound from my mother—sounds I had never heard before. I stood, feet frozen, unable to breathe, wanting to get away but unable to move, listening to those sounds from the other side of the door while my bladder relentlessly pressed. I caught sight of myself in the full-length mirror opposite the stairs—a mop-haired, bug-eyed kid in blue striped pajamas, who looked as though he thought someone was about to smack him. It broke the spell. I fled to the bathroom and stayed there for half an hour.

After that, I began to notice things around the house that must have always been there but had never come to my attention. There was the large blue-and-white box of Kotex that sat on a high shelf in the bathroom and the bloody remains in the bathroom garbage. The box of condoms that I found tucked in under my father's socks while rooting for loose change in his dresser one afternoon gave me the best evidence so far that my parents were, in fact, having sex. I knew about condoms from Ernie, but it was my mother who told me about the Kotex.

I came pounding into the bathroom one afternoon on a Saturday to get a long, sucking drink of water from the tap, only to find my mother taking down that blue-and-white box from the shelf. I watched, transfixed, as she actually began to explain to me what the pads were for. It felt like a hand was squeezing my throat. She told me about a woman's cycle and that the Kotex was to catch the blood during menstruation. I couldn't get out of there fast enough.

In the weeks that followed, I began avoiding my parents, not wanting any more lessons in human physiology. I was confused and upset, and I was in retreat. It wasn't difficult to avoid my father, given how much the man worked and how tired he was by the end of the day. My mother, on the other hand, was harder to avoid. Not wanting her to ask me unwanted questions, or to offer me unwelcome information, or even to think something was wrong, I didn't give either her or my dad the chance to corner me. Confused, upset, and wanting not to see these things in my own home, I spent most of that winter saying as little as possible to my parents.

But it wasn't just the books on human reproduction miraculously appearing around the house that helped to keep me in retreat. These were tasteful books: some with illustrations showing the male and female anatomy, some with photographs of women in labour or nursing mothers, some with both illustrations and photographs of babies. Whatever their configuration, these books always had education as their aim and babies as their result. I would sometimes find one of these books on the coffee table under a magazine or stuck at the bottom of a pile of other books. I never read them, but I would look at the pictures if no one was around: pictures of nursing babies or women squatting to give birth just didn't fit with what I knew of life in Galahad.

It wouldn't have been so bad if it had just been trying to fend off my mother and her crusade on reproductive education, but something else was happening to me that was baffling and distressing. I began noticing women: how they looked, how they smelled, what they wore, how they walked. Seeing a woman would make my head turn, just like a dog nosing a scent. I felt weird about it, but I looked and looked. I knew everybody in town, of course, so it was embarrassing when someone caught me looking. The feeling didn't discriminate by age or anything else, either. I would find myself looking at high school girls in short jackets and tight jeans, and then watching Mrs. Perkins, solidly forty who helped run the Petro-Can at the end of Main, with her broad hips and arms bared to the shoulders in the sleeveless sweatshirts she always seemed to wear. To my complete discomfiture, the feeling even seemed to extend to my own mother.

One afternoon, I was sitting at the desk in the living room flipping through a Batman comic when my mother came home from work. She was dressed up and was even wearing lipstick. As I looked up from my comic, I saw that she was lovely, with her fogged glasses in her hand, and her skin pink and glowing from the February afternoon—not that I put it that way to myself, or even understood it at the time.

I never told any of this to Ernie, of course. He would have laughed his head off and made gagging noises if he had heard me talking about looking at my own mother that way. And anyway, Ernie had his own way of looking at women.

Ernie's dad had a shelf full of *Playboys* in the basement, right above the five-foot fish tank that was full of exotic-looking, multicoloured fish, strange rocks, and fake sea plants. Ernie's dad wasn't around much. He owned Galahad's nine-hole golf course, and he ran the curling rink in the winter. Sometimes Ernie needed to talk to his dad after school, and we would wander into the rink, which stunk of stale tobacco smoke, coffee, and old shoes. We would watch the curlers through the glass awhile before going upstairs to find Ernie's dad at the bar. His response to seeing us was always the same.

"What the hell are you kids hanging around here for?"

Ernie's dad was a tall, thin man, hatchet-faced, with clumsy, restless hands that seemed unused to the suit he always wore. Ernie always protested that we weren't hanging around, while I watched the movements of those hands. After giving us hell, he would answer whatever Ernie had to ask, and then always end with, "Now I don't want you kids hanging around here. This isn't the goddamn arcade."

That was Ernie's dad. And with him hardly ever being around, and Ernie's mom working at the post office, we had plenty of opportunities to explore the *Playboys*. It wasn't as though I didn't want to look; I was as curious as Ernie. We would spread out six or eight issues on the floor, and Ernie would guffaw and catcall over what he found. I joined in, but there was something cold gripping my belly the whole time we looked. Some of the pictures were shadowy, but most simply had women in various poses, sitting, lying, or standing, showing breasts, hips, and legs. What I didn't understand were the expressions on the women's faces. It wasn't as though I expected them to be smiling, but these were expressions I had never seen before.

One picture that held my attention was of a woman sitting on a chair, holding a bouquet of flowers beneath her breasts with a blanket spread over her lap. The photo was brightly lit, and the woman filled the entire page. Her breasts were heavy, with long, dark pink nipples, and she was staring straight at the camera. Her light brown hair was pulled back into a bun at the top and back of her head, and long strands fell over her shoulders. I found it hard to look away from her. Her face was oval-shaped and calm, the eyes looking at me with an implacability I couldn't read.

"She ain't so great," said Ernie, leaning over to look at the picture. "What you looking at her for? Here's something special." And he flapped open the centerfold to the magazine he was holding…It went like that all winter, me trying to make sense of everything at home and at school and looking at *Playboys* in Ernie's basement.

On a day in March when the sun was bright and the ground was patchy with the remains of winter snow, Ernie caught up to me after school. He was grinning behind his glasses, and I knew that meant he had a plan.

"We got to make a trip to Ed's," he said, still grinning.

"Ed's," I said. "What for?"

"Because we're going to go to work for Ed."

"What for?" I said again. "Ernie, I got to go home."

"So go home. I'll pick you up on the way."

"I don't know if my mom'll let me."

"Don't be such a goddamn baby. You gotta tell mommy everything? Tell her we're just going to the store."

I didn't have an answer, so I headed across Main and up the street to my house. My mother wasn't home, and there was a note on the table saying she would be back at five. This left me no excuse but to tag along after Ernie in whatever he was planning. The feed shop, as I said, was at the end of the road running out past the hospital. We could get to it easily enough just by following the road that bordered the field by my house until we came to the hospital road that ran west out of town.

"So why we got to go see Ed?" I asked, kicking at the road resentfully.

"Listen," said Ernie. "You want to make some money, right?"

"I guess so."

"You guess so. Listen, peckerhead. Ed pays cash for stuff. We can find stuff he wants, and sell it to him."

The idea was intriguing. "What kind of stuff?" I asked, feeling sure that neither of my parents would approve.

"I don' know." Ernie waved his arms impatiently. "We got to see what he has and what he wants."

We went along like that, me kicking rocks in the road, and Ernie going on about what he was going to buy with all the money we made, until we came to the feed shop and found Ed sitting behind a makeshift desk, looking at a magazine that he hurriedly shoved under the counter when we walked in.

"Help you, boys?" he said, leaning back in his chair and eyeing us balefully. Ed was a tall, raw-boned man, with bad teeth and a long jaw. He pulled a pouch of tobacco from his shirt pocket and absently began to roll a cigarette while he watched us out of cat-green eyes.

Ernie and I looked at each other. I saw with some satisfaction that Ernie was looking pale behind his glasses. "We were wondering," said Ernie. "We were wondering if we could work for you."

Ed gave a short, barking laugh. "What the hell do you think I am, kid?" He waved a hand around the room. "This place look like I could hire an extra hand?"

I looked around. It was a large, dusty room, with perhaps a dozen shelves standing in rows, all jumbled with an assortment of feed for dogs and horses and other junk I couldn't identify.

"I don't need no assistant," said Ed. He leaned to the side, snorted, and then spat into an old ice cream bucket on the floor. Then he leaned back again and lit a thin cigarette.

"No," said Ernie, mustering his composure. "Not for in here. We thought we could find stuff for you, stuff you could use or sell. Then you could pay us for what we brought in."

Ed stared hard at Ernie. "And just how much am I supposed to pay you?"

"That depends." Ernie was recovering himself quickly. "We bring in stuff that we think you might want to buy, and then we negotiate."

"Negotiate," said Ed, with another of his barking laughs. "Well ain't you the cat's ass." But I could see that Ernie had his attention. "I don't take just anything," he said, looking at me and then back to Ernie. "You can bring stuff in, but I ain't sayin' I'll buy it." He looked back to me. "You're Ray's kid, ain't you?" I nodded my head. "Ray's a good shit," said Ed, dragging on his cigarette and staring up at the ceiling. He blew out a long stream of smoke and seemed to make a decision. "You boys bring me something you think I can use. If I like it, I'll give you something for it." He looked at me again. "You might start by seeing if your old man has some car parts he wouldn't mind gettin' rid of."

That was how Ernie and I came to work for Ed. He was a lousy boss, and we spent most of our free time scavenging the town for junk.

Sometimes he paid and sometimes he didn't. He always pretended not to care, but he always looked over what we brought in with a critical eye. And we brought in everything we could find.

Our first acquisitions were fairly modest. Ernie tried to convince me to go down to my dad's station and see what we could get.

"I don't know," I said.

"Come on," said Ernie. "Ed told us to ask your dad about parts."

"What do we tell him if he asks why we want them?"

"Nothin'."

"He'll ask."

"Who gives a shit? If he asks we tell him we need the stuff 'cause we want to build ourselves a engine."

I laughed at this, but Ernie was right. My dad asked why we wanted parts, but he seemed to accept our halfhearted story about wanting to build an engine—maybe because he just wanted to get rid of us. He told us we could have anything we found in the shed.

The shed was attached to the back of the garage, and it was dark and smelled of rust and old grease. We rummaged around until we found an old car radio, a set of springs—only slightly rusted—and a boxlike thing that I couldn't identify.

"We need more than this," said Ernie. "He'll think we're just a couple kids." I didn't bother to point out to Ernie that we were a couple of kids, and Ed would probably laugh us out of his feed shop no matter what we brought.

We persisted for two days. After school, we got on our bikes and combed the town. We didn't actually find a whole lot more, but it was something of an education to see what people threw away. Even Ernie was surprised when we discovered the copies of *Penthouse* bundled up with the old newspapers behind the Baptist church. We tried not to be obvious about what we were doing because we both had the feeling that people would be upset if they knew we had been pulling apart their garbage to look for stuff to sell to Ed. But it was junk. People were throwing it away, so how could it matter? At least that's what I told myself.

Ed seemed to think so, too, but he was less generous in his estimation of our haul of stuff. "Just what the hell am I s'posed to do with this crap?" he said, surveying the assortment of things we had laid out on his table. Ernie was red behind his glasses. Ed stared at us and rolled a cigarette. "If you boys want me to pay you for stuff, then you got to do better than this. Now get this shit outta here."

That's how it went for most of March and April—Ernie and me bringing stuff in to Ed, and Ed alternately jeering or praising us for what we had found. I never quite got over the sense that we were doing something wrong, but most of the time what we found or took was just junk other people didn't want anyway. We brought a slightly rusted jack, two usable, if worn, tires, a perfectly good straight-backed wooden chair, an old black-and-white television, at least three radios, and other assorted junk that Ed glanced at once and told us to get out of his shop.

There were a surprising number of magazines, the kind Ernie's dad kept in his basement. These Ed kept for himself. "You boys old enough to know what a tit is?" Ed would ask, flipping open one of the magazines for us to see. I never said anything, but Ernie would look at the magazine and then stare up at Ed. "That ain't so great." And Ed would laugh his barking laugh until he doubled over coughing and spat into the ice cream pail beside the desk.

What it meant for both of us was pocket money. We spent it on pop or chips, and once Ernie even managed to convince Mrs. Davenport at the drugstore that his dad needed cigarettes. She looked doubtful as she handed over the cigarettes and the change, but Ernie just looked up at her in that wide-eyed way he had that put most people at ease. I never did tell my parents what we were doing. I liked the money, and after a while I was as dedicated as Ernie about keeping an eye out for stuff that we could sell to Ed.

One of our biggest finds was a set of storm windows that the hospital was getting rid of, but it was also the one that pushed Ernie to his limit. We endured Ed's scoffing and his sarcasm because he paid us, and as despicable as he was, Ed was an adult. As kids, we had a tacit understanding that adults held the supreme authority, and some were just better about it than others. I always figured most adults simply tolerated kids as a necessary evil.

There were more than two dozen windows stacked at the back of the hospital ready for removal. For some reason, this felt more like stealing than anything else we had taken to that point. We brought one of the windows in to show Ed.

"Where the hell d'you get this?"

"Lots more like it where that came from," said Ernie, staring stubbornly back at Ed.

Ed looked at Ernie and then at me with an expression I couldn't read. "You bring in what you have, and I'll give you a buck a piece for 'em."

And that was that. There were nearly three dozen storms for us to grab, and we headed off to bring in our haul. But when we looked at those stacks of windows, even Ernie admitted that we needed some help. "I'll call my cousin Bo," he said. "He can bring his dad's truck."

Bo, I knew, was one of the Rimbey kids. When I hesitated, Ernie said he would just tell Bo that we had permission to take the windows. Bo was willing to help—for ten dollars. But that was okay, because when it was all said and done, Ernie and I would have twenty-four dollars to split between us.

It seemed a small fortune. I was hardly ever able to wheedle more than a dollar out of my dad at any one time, so fourteen dollars all at once was like Christmas. I was sitting on the back steps reading a brand-new Batman comic when Ernie banged open the back gate. He was on his bike, and he dumped it on the grass and came walking up the sidewalk to where I was sitting. He looked mad.

"You know what that prick did?"

I wasn't sure at first who the prick was, but I felt a clenching in my stomach at Ernie's tone.

"He sold those windows to a guy over in Bruce for five bucks apiece. Five bucks!"

I stared.

"Don't you get it?"

I was still trying to sort out why Ernie was so mad. "That's a lot," I said cautiously, after a minute.

"Fuckin' right it's a lot. He ripped us off. We're the ones who found those storms, and we're the ones who brought them in."

"How do you know?"

"Bo. He was talking to Ed, and the prick was bragging about what he'd done. Bo thought it was hilarious."

I still didn't understand. Ed was an adult, and we were just kids. He could do what he wanted.

Ernie flopped down on the bottom step and kicked at the grass savagely. "I feel like going over there."

"Where?"

"Ed's, you idiot."

"And do what?"

He didn't seem to have an answer for that, but he got to his feet and looked at me. "I don't know about you, but I'm not going to be screwed by that asshole Ed Jenkins."

I didn't see Ernie outside of school for almost a week. The following Saturday was the beginning of May, and my mom was going into town. As soon as she was out of the house, I headed for Ed's. I figured that Ernie might be there, and I was right. There he was, standing in the yard, looking smug and watching Ed unscrewing the rear license plate from a Plymouth. The car was new, or at least I had never seen it in Ed's yard before. It was white, and the sides were spattered with mud.

Ed looked up as I walked across the yard. "Whatcha want, kid?"

I stopped and looked over at Ernie, but he didn't say anything. "Just looking for Ernie," I said.

Ed finished with the license plate and picked up a second from the ground. He stood and looked at me and then Ernie. "Well," he finally said, "you boys want to be useful, then you can start by washing this car." He turned and walked toward the house. "Buckets and rags in the shed," he called back over his shoulder.

I looked a question at Ernie, but he just shrugged his shoulders. He waited until Ed was inside his house and then pulled open the driver's door.

"Whose car?" I asked.

"Don't know. Think Ed wants to sell it, though."

"Who's car?" I said again.

Ernie turned around and stared at me from the front seat. He scuffed his shoes on the gravel and looked away. When he looked back the smirk was gone.

"If you tell anybody, I'll kill you."

"Tell what?"

"I found it."

"The car?"

"Yeah. Down there by the Hampton place. Near the marsh. Keys in it and everything."

"You stole it?"

"Didn't steal it. Jesus Christ. Somebody just left it there."

I didn't say anything.

Ernie craned his neck to see the house through the passenger window. "Figured we should have a look inside before he comes back." Ernie pulled the keys from the ignition and slid off the seat. He walked to the rear and fitted a key to the trunk lock. He looked at me with a grin and then popped the trunk.

I could see Ernie's face turn from chalk white to a pale green as he stared into the trunk. Then he began to back away. I stepped forward to look and met a pair of vacant blue eyes staring back at me out of a face whose mouth was drawn down into a grimace. I had the impression of blood and matted hair, of one naked arm and breast, and of discoloured skin half-concealed by a dirty pink blanket.

I felt as though somebody had punched me in the stomach. My head was buzzing, and I suddenly couldn't see anything but dots and swirls of colour. My knees gave way. I could hear the sound of retching and then a shout from somewhere behind me.

I struggled to my feet and ran. I never looked back. I ran all the way home, not really feeling the ground under my feet but hearing the whole time a strange animal noise that I knew afterward must have been the sound of my own voice.

It wasn't until long after my mom got home from town, and after she had called my dad at the garage, that they found me, hiding under the basement stairs. I must have gabbled out the story, but I don't remember making any sense. There were other phone calls after that. My mom made me go to bed, and I could hear the sound of voices for a long time. There was some shouting for a while, but after a time everything was still. In the stillness I heard footsteps on the stairs. My eyes were tightly shut, but I knew it was my mother. She didn't say a word. She just sat down on the edge of my bed and rubbed her hand up and down my back until I could begin to let go of what I had been holding since that morning.

The woman we found in the trunk of the white Plymouth was twenty-two-year-old Mary Oliver from Calgary. She had apparently been visiting relatives in Edmonton when she was abducted on the Thursday night before we found her. These were the facts as my parents gave them to me once I had the courage to ask the questions.

It is years later that I find myself in the library archives, hunting through old copies of the newspaper to find something of that young woman.

I find a small article dated May 10, 1976. The body of Mary Oliver, born 1954, was discovered in the trunk of a car abandoned outside the city. Miss Oliver is survived by two sisters, Rebecca and Charlotte, and parents, Michael and Susan. Mary had just completed the first year of a bachelor of arts degree at the University of Alberta, and she was only staying for a few days with an aunt and uncle in Edmonton before going on to a summer job in Jasper. Her killer was one Larry Bench, thirty-nine years old and formerly of Edmonton. He was in custody, facing charges of abduction, sexual assault, and first-degree murder.

I wonder about the job Mary was going to in Jasper, and what she was going to do once she finished university. I try to imagine the things she may have liked, if she read, if she got along with her family.

But at the time, I didn't want to know anything. My parents seemed to accept my explanation that Ernie and I were going to wash the car for Ed when we discovered Mary's body, and nobody seemed to find out that Ernie and I had been selling stuff to Ed. Ed managed to talk his way out of trouble, and apart from school I only ever saw Ernie once before my family moved to the city. We never spoke; he just looked at me as he came out of the post office with his dad before climbing into the cab of their truck and slamming the door.

I don't remember much else from that spring and summer save the move. A kind of fog had settled over my brain. My family left Galahad at the beginning of August. My parents must have told me what was happening, and in some way my brain registered that my dad had sold the garage and that we were moving to the city. The movers came; the house was emptied. We stuffed the car with odds and ends, pillows and suitcases. I wedged myself into the backseat, and we took Main Street out of town. I looked back only once. My dad pulled the car onto the highway and I peered over the tops of suitcases to see the town disappearing in the distance, sliding away from me into the heat-haze of the August afternoon, as though it were being set adrift on an unsettled sea, a fragment of space and time left to find its own way in a world that I no longer wanted and willed to leave behind forever.

TRANSFORMATIONS

Aunt Nora had a way of making her presence felt through the entire house. She ran things with efficiency and organization, fueling everyone around her with the fire of her enthusiasm and guiding them with the strength of her will. For Josselyn, having moved to Edmonton at the end of harvest and experiencing city life for the first time, Aunt Nora's personality was a little overwhelming. Even though Aunt Nora was so unlike her own father, she was family, and Josselyn felt comforted by the sense that she was on familiar ground, and that this was a game she already knew how to play.

Aunt Nora and her father were the kind of people who took it for granted that the rest of the world would simply follow along in their wakes, but the similarities stopped there. Josselyn always found it difficult to imagine them growing up in the same house, or why they continued to see each other at Easter and Christmas. Each dismissed the other's lifestyle, and neither would acknowledge the other; they simply talked at and around each other in an odd dance of words that never amounted to much of anything.

Just after Easter, with the end of high school in sight, Josselyn had phoned Aunt Nora to ask if she could stay with her and Uncle Paul the next October, until she was able to find a job and an apartment. "Of course," had been the robust reply. "I'll get Paul to work on finishing the basement room. It was going to be Sarah's, but you can have it until you've got a place of your own." Josselyn was uncertain how cousin

Sarah would feel about the arrangement, but she hoped it would only be until Christmas. Josselyn knew Aunt Nora well enough not to argue, so she hung up the phone with a quick prayer that she was doing the right thing.

The trick at Aunt Nora's, as it had been at home, was staying out of the way, but that was easier said than done, despite the spacious first and second floors and mostly finished basement. Keeping track of who was who in the house was itself a challenge. In Nora's immediate orbit were the cousins: eight-year-old David and twelve-year-old Sarah. Beyond them was Uncle Paul, bulky and reassuring; then came Beth, Aunt Nora's friend, with Charles, Beth's shadowy boyfriend, who seemed always in the background.

Aunt Nora usually referred to Beth and Charles in the singular. "Beth-and-Charles," she told Josselyn the first day, "are in the house for a while. Beth is recovering." Recovering from what, Aunt Nora didn't explain.

There were the pets, too: George, a black Lab; Sally, a Jack Russell terrier; and a cat, Milo. Aunt Nora's wider orbit included an unending stream of friends and acquaintances, most of whom came and went regularly, sometimes coming in for coffee or tea but often just standing by the door to chat for a few minutes.

With all of this humanity and livestock, Josselyn was hard-pressed at first to know how to fit in. She had a sense that if you wanted to fall within Aunt Nora's circle of attention, it was necessary to figure out who held what favour and why, and then try to maintain your own. It was never really a case of trying to please Aunt Nora; she made up her mind about people regardless of what they did or didn't do, which sometimes meant that she made her decision before she even met them. One thing was for certain—Nora was never in any doubt as to how she felt about anyone. If there was a difference between being around Aunt Nora and her own father, it was the complexity of Nora's network, and this, on top of being four months out of high school and intent on getting a job in the city, was more than enough to make Josselyn feel anxious about the move.

After finishing her grade twelve in June, Josselyn had been increasingly desperate to leave the farm. Ellie, Josselyn's stepmother, was a born-again Christian evangelist, and the two of them had stopped getting along after Josselyn had started junior high.

Grade seven was hard for Josselyn. While other girls were wearing bras and getting their periods, Josselyn stayed tall, bustless, and nonhormonal.

She had complained once to Ellie that she hadn't yet got her rags. It was a word some of the girls at school used. Josselyn knew it would provoke her stepmother, but she said it anyway. It did. Ellie was spitting with anger as she yelled at Josselyn. It was worse than after Ellie had discovered a Stephen King novel in Josselyn's bedroom.

"This is evil," she had screamed at Josselyn, holding up the book, her face white and the corners of her mouth foaming. After that, Josselyn kept the books she thought would make her stepmother crazy in her locker at school.

When she finally got her first period, she told her father, not Ellie. Her father was watching television in the living room, leaning back tiredly in the big La-Z-Boy. He always looked slightly out of place in the living room, carefully decorated with Ellie's knickknacks and doilies.

Josselyn perched on the arm of his chair. "I got my period, finally," she said.

Her father looked up with a tired smile. "That's good," he said, and patted her knee.

For her father, this was simply information, and Josselyn knew it. Sometimes she thought her father saw her in the same way as he did the animals on the farm. It was all just biology to him.

Josselyn sometimes fantasized about what such conversations would be like with her own mother. She would look at Josselyn, smile, and then hug her close. But Josselyn had more trouble with the conversation itself. She'd never had such a talk with her own mother. Carol had left when Josselyn was not quite two years old.

Ellie, unlike her father, was concerned about Josselyn's soul. She didn't want Josselyn running with the wrong crowd in high school. She didn't want Josselyn getting involved with boys, or drugs, or anything of the outside world that would put Josselyn's soul in jeopardy. It was always her soul—never Josselyn herself.

Josselyn learned early to construct the truth in a particular way, creating a fiction of acceptable friends and activities throughout her high school years. Ellie questioned her closely, but Josselyn's fiction held—for the most part. It wasn't that hard. She never had a steady boyfriend; she only got drunk twice and tried weed once. She never slept around, unlike some girls who would spread their legs for anyone. Josselyn never did. She had a crowd—sort of—but she was never at the center of things, always an outsider in a way that she never understood.

Ellie was horrified when Josselyn announced that she was going to the city to live with Aunt Nora. Ellie had been quick to point out *that heathen woman*, as she called Aunt Nora, would do Josselyn no good, and if anything would corrupt her soul. Her father was less prepared to argue with Josselyn.

"She can go if she wants," he'd said to Ellie flatly while the two of them stared at each other across the kitchen. Josselyn was standing uncomfortably by the table.

"Besides," her father said, "Nora is family, and that's a good thing."

For her father, it always came down to family. He might not speak to Nora for months at a time, but she was family, and that was enough for him.

"Just don't forget about us here," he said as they pulled up in front of the Galahad bus depot, squeezed into one end of Holten's Hardware. This was as far as Josselyn would let him take her, insisting that she could ride the bus into town, and that Nora could pick her up at the south side terminal.

"But I can just drive you to Nora's," her father said, hauling the large cardboard box, securely bound with packing tape, out of the back of the pickup. Josselyn refused for the fifth time. And without another word, her father wedged himself and the box through the doorway into the depot, while Josselyn followed with two heavy suitcases. Fifteen minutes later, she was sitting on the bus while it ground its way out of town and onto the highway, passing newly stubbled fields on its way to the city.

The bus ride into the city had been disappointingly short; she barely felt she was going anywhere, but at least she had been on her own. Nora met her at the south side stop, and as they drove back to the house, Nora filled her in on everything that had happened since the previous Easter.

That first afternoon at Aunt Nora's had been quiet. Beth and Charles had been resting, and Josselyn kept glancing nervously at the closed door of the room along the hall. Aunt Nora took her around the house, as the last time that Josselyn had visited her aunt and uncle they had been living on the north side. This house was large and airy, with hardwood floors and wide windows. They wandered into the back bedroom and Aunt Nora showed her the meditation room. A wide shelf against one wall held everything from an assortment of rocks, to a long black feather and a Tibetan singing bowl. Aunt Nora touched the things on the shelf, explaining how she had come by each one. Josselyn knew her aunt was *different*, as her stepmother would say, but most of this was new to Josselyn, and she looked at everything with curiosity.

Aunt Nora also did much of her art here. A folding table was set up in the center of the floor and covered with a mass of fabric and other odds and ends. On the back wall of the room was a large triangular-shaped weaving. Josselyn stared at it, not knowing what to think or to say. It hung point downward, a blend of red, yellow, and black wool surrounding an opening that was divided by a thick braid of red.

Aunt Nora was looking at it intently. "I made this," she said, "after a goddess workshop I attended two years ago. I spent the whole winter on it. It was very satisfying to make."

There was a pause while the two of them stood in silent appreciation of the weaving. Josselyn was unaccountably reminded of a calfskin that she had hung on her bedroom wall at the farm. The winter she had turned twelve one of the cows had given birth to a stillborn calf. It had been a hard labour for the cow, a smallish Guernsey, and Josselyn had stayed in the barn with her father while the cow laboured, groaning and blowing, the smell of blood and shit heavy on the air. When the calf was finally born, it lay curled on the rough boards of the floor while the cow nosed it, and her father watched, his face set and closed.

When Josselyn had asked him what he was going to do with the calf, he looked at her in surprise. "Do with it?" he asked. "Why?"

"I want the hide," said Josselyn, half-hopeful and half-embarrassed.

Her father looked at her for a long time, as though he were judging the weight and worth of an animal at the auction mart, and then he slowly nodded his head. "All right," he said. "You can have the hide." And her father sighed, running his hand over the cow's flank while it continued to nose the dead calf. Josselyn had felt a flush of pleasure, more at the look than at her father's agreement. That look meant approval, and such approval was dear to Josselyn.

That afternoon, they had skinned out the calf, her father showing her how to use the knife and scrape the hide. She cured it, and then tacked it to the wall above her bed. The hide had eventually made its way into the basement, but she always remembered the look from her father whenever she saw the calfskin hanging above her bed.

Remembering all of this while she stood in Aunt Nora's meditation room seemed rather odd, but she knew that approval from Aunt Nora was as important as it had been from her father.

Josselyn reached out and touched the end of the braid. "I like it," she said.

Aunt Nora smiled. "I guess all of this isn't really what you're used to."

Josselyn laughed, slightly embarrassed. "I guess," she said. "It's different from home, but that's okay. I mostly wanted a change, anyway, maybe work for a year before going back to school." It was the story she told curious adults.

Aunt Nora nodded absently, and then led Josselyn out of the meditation room. After showing her the rest of the house, Aunt Nora took her down to the basement. She apologized for the state of the room. Josselyn didn't really mind that the walls were unpainted, or that her door was only an old curtain. At least it was out of the way and she could always escape to the basement if she was feeling overwhelmed.

Josselyn spent that first week settling in to life at Aunt Nora's. Everyone and everything in the house had a function, and from what Josselyn could see, even though Aunt Nora was so much like her own father, Paul was the only one who approached anything like what she was used to in her own life. He was a quiet man, with thinning brown hair and gentle eyes, and in spite of seeming to hang so much in the background, Josselyn recognized and liked his quiet strength. Paul got the kids to school every morning and returned late afternoon or early evening. He was an assistant professor in the English department at the university. Sometimes Josselyn would come upstairs in the evening after David and Sarah were in bed to find him sitting at the long dining room table with papers and books spread before him. He seemed to be always marking essays and exams from his classes at the university.

All in all, Josselyn liked being at Aunt Nora's. It was different than what she was used to, but she found it curiously comforting. There were books everywhere, but most were not the kind of thing she would ever find at home: the novels, yes, but not the books on crystals, homeopathy, or home birth. Aunt Nora's art that found temporary spots all over the house, the meals that included tofu or soy, the very noticeable lack of a television, were all different from home, but a welcome change from her father's silences and her stepmother's preaching.

At the end of the first week, Josselyn stands dutifully chopping tomato and celery at the kitchen counter for the customary supper salad, while the household goes on around her. Four o'clock and both kids are home from school: David coming the two blocks from the elementary, while Sarah having the longer walk from the junior high. Both cousins are trying to tell their mother about their day at the same time. Beth, looking pale and willowy as ever, has emerged from her afternoon nap, and Charles—her significant other, as Nora likes to call him—is hanging about the kitchen looking concerned and getting in the way.

"I just wish I felt well enough to try and help," Beth says for what must be the twentieth time.

My god.

Nora's eyes become hard as she bends over the open door to the oven to check a large pan of vegetarian lasagna. She determinedly closes the oven door and sets the mitts down on the counter with a precision that is as good as a warning.

Josselyn turns back to her cutting board hastily. She picks up a long English cucumber, shreds away the plastic, and looks at it momentarily dismayed. Should she peel it or not? At home, she would have never bothered, but here she is uncertain, given Nora's attitude toward nonorganic food. She shoots a furtive glance at Aunt Nora.

"Why don't you and Charles go into the living room and pick some music," Aunt Nora says to Beth in a sweetly controlled voice that Josselyn recognizes as the second indication that Aunt Nora is losing her cool.

Peeled, she thinks, quickly turning back to the cutting board as Sarah and David disappear into the living room. Just then the doorbell rings, setting off a chorus of bays and yaps from George and Sally.

"Paul will be home in a few minutes," Nora says over the noise. "I asked him to stop in at Earthworks. The food order's in today, and when he gets here, Charles, you can help him bring it in."

Aunt Nora was the dedicated director and scheduler of the family. She organized everyone's time, writing everything down in a small book that went with her everywhere. She regulated the food in the house, doling out healthy snacks to the kids after school. She didn't believe in sugar, white flour, or anything that came in a tin. She wasn't opposed to alcohol, but only wine, and only in carefully measured portions. She had even offered Josselyn a glass of red one evening, which made Josselyn feel like an adult as she reached out a hand to take the stemmed glass, and like a kid for wanting to spit out her first mouthful.

After a couple of weeks, Josselyn began to realize that Nora didn't quite have the control over the household she had first thought. Emptying out David's backpack one day after school, Josselyn found a stash of candy. Vacuuming Sarah's room, she discovered two plastic Coca-Cola empties under the bed, and hunting for a hammer and nail in Uncle Paul's workshop, she discovered a glass and bottle of scotch on a lower shelf.

But the contraband in sugar and alcohol wasn't the most notable thing about the house. The oddest thing was Beth-and-Charles. They were in the house only temporarily, but neither seemed in a hurry to go anywhere. "Beth is a channeler," Aunt Nora had explained in that first week, "and she's had a rough time." Josselyn hadn't a clue what a channeler was, but she gathered from a number of conversations that Beth spoke to spirits or something from the other side. Beth seemed older than Aunt Nora, but Charles had to be ten or fifteen years younger. Charles was Beth's support and, as far as Josselyn could see, had no other function but to follow Beth around looking supportive. He was a paler shadow of Beth's shadowy self, and Josselyn sometimes had trouble making a distinction between the two of them—until she caught Charles looking at her.

It was furtive, at first. He would be sitting or standing next to Beth, looking as weakly supportive as ever, and then Josselyn would surprise a glance from his direction. This happened again and again. While clearing the table one evening after dinner, she looked up to meet his sad, washed-out eyes watching her. She stared right back, and he looked away nervously, bunching his hands in his lap.

Only once since Josselyn's arrival had she even seen Charles in a different room from Beth. The second Saturday after her arrival in the house, Josselyn had been making pancakes for David and Sarah. Nora and Paul were both out of the house, and Josselyn nearly jumped out of her skin when she looked up from the frying pan to suddenly see Charles standing in the doorway.

"Can I help?" he asked. He looked detached, somehow, standing there with his pale hair brushed straight back from his forehead and still damp from the shower.

Josselyn had noticed that he always had a slightly washed-out, greasy, colourless look, in spite of showering as many as three times a day. His hair, like Beth's, was so pale it was almost white, and his eyes were such a faded blue they were nearly gray. He was smiling slightly and trying to look friendly, which put Josselyn even more on the defensive. He wore a sweater that Josselyn had seen on Beth, and around his neck hung a pendant in the shape of the Yin Yang symbol that Beth had been wearing on Josselyn's first evening in the house.

What the hell was with that?

"Can I help with something?" he asked again, edging farther into the kitchen.

"No," Josselyn said, a little too quickly. She looked down to see if the pancakes had begun to bubble in the pan, and then back up at Charles. He looked hurt, and Josselyn bit her lip, remembering what Aunt Nora had said about feelings as part of Josselyn's introduction to the household: "Feelings," she had said, "are precious."

"You could get some plates for David and Sarah," said Josselyn, still speaking too quickly. "And for you, too—if you would like some pancakes."

Charles meekly went to the cupboard. He took down plates, a bottle of organic maple syrup, and set the items on the counter. Josselyn tried not to look at Charles as he paced silently in and out of the kitchen, carefully arranging the table with plates, cutlery, a dish of butter, and the syrup, and looking generally mournful and eager to please. Fortunately, Aunt Nora exploded into the house just as they were sitting down to eat, and Josselyn looked up with relief at her aunt, the picture of vitality in her jeans and heavy Cowichan sweater, with her cheeks and eyes bright from the cool October morning. Charles did not make another attempt to engage her, but after that Josselyn sometimes felt uneasy about the curtain that served as her bedroom door. It wouldn't exactly stop anyone who wanted to come in.

It is nearly December before Josselyn finds work—thirty hours a week at Trailers, one of the video stores on the Avenue. At the end of her first week at the store, Josselyn looks up to see snow thickly swirling against the windows. The door opens, and Sharif, the other full-timer, comes in followed by a gust of wintry air and a spray of snow. Sharif is a twentysomething hipster—not that he would ever call himself that. He tells Josselyn about movies she needs to watch, never failing to show dismay over what she hasn't seen. She keeps a list under the counter, and she watches them during her shift. He is always pleased if he arrives to find her watching one of his picks. Josselyn doesn't bother to tell him which ones she hates.

At 3:00, she grabs her coat, says goodbye to Sharif, and hurries out into the fading afternoon. She is without hat or gloves, and she shoves her hands into her coat pockets and blinks away the flakes that swirl into her face and obscure traffic. It's easier to think of Aunt Nora's as home now, but she knows the next step is looking for an apartment of her own.

She walks down the Avenue, feeling the glow of working and of going home, and peering into shop windows as she passes. Inside, people are removed from the weather, seemingly more distant as they cluster around counters, coats hanging open, and red-faced from the artificial indoor heat.

Josselyn hurries past the Safeway and turns down a side street that will take her back to Aunt Nora's. As she walks, she watches the world change in the swirling air; dead leaves are rapidly disappearing beneath the snow, and her shoes make a muffled scrape on the sidewalk.

The steps up to the front door are covered with a thickening layer of snow. It squeaks and crunches underfoot as Josselyn pushes her way into the house. It's quiet, and Josselyn hangs up her coat in the hall closet, hearing the sound of the shower as she passes the bathroom on her way to the kitchen. There is a note tacked to the cupboard, and Josselyn leans forward to read it:

"Josselyn," it begins, in Aunt Nora's firm script, "left casserole in fridge. Could you please put in oven at four o'clock (350 dgs). And wake Beth at 3:30. She has appointment on Avenue at 5:00. Will be home at 4:30 to pick her up. Love, AN."

It's three thirty now. Josselyn puts down the note with a sigh and marches down the hall to Beth-and-Charles's room. The door is ajar, and Josselyn reaches out to knock before changing her mind and unceremoniously pushing back the door in pure defiance of Aunt Nora's rule about respecting other people's space in the house. Josselyn is fed up with both of them and hopes they will find a place soon—before they drive everyone in the house crazy. Beth's dramatic wounded presence is tiresome, and Charles's puppy dog way of following her about the house is just irritating.

The figure that stands in the center of the room has its back to Josselyn, the hair loose about its neck, the strap of a flesh-coloured bra dark against the colourless skin. Josselyn is about to step back with an apology when the figure turns.

The hair is brushed straight back from the forehead, and the faded blue, almost gray eyes rivet Josselyn to where she stands, causing her to stare back in appalling recognition.

Charles.

The mute, naked appeal in the faded eyes finds an echo in the soft lines of his face.

"I love you," he says, his eyes never wavering from hers.

Josselyn feels her chest throb with emotion. She had mostly avoided Charles since arriving at Aunt Nora's, and now here he is, dressed in Beth's underwear, and telling her that he loves her. It's ludicrous. But she also feels an awkward, half-ashamed compassion for this man who has given himself away so completely. She takes a breath and, following an impulse, she steps forward, reaches out her hand, and presses her palm firmly against his forehead. It's a gesture she's seen her father use when trying to calm an agitated or hurt animal. Charles leans into her palm and closes his eyes. After a suspended moment, feeling the pressure of his forehead against her palm and hearing his slow exhalation of breath, she slowly withdraws her hand. Charles stands, still leaning forward, his eyes closed, a rapt expression on his face.

"You'd better get dressed," says Josselyn. "Beth's out of the shower, and Sarah and David will be home any minute." And then she turns and leaves the room.

After supper that evening, Josselyn helps Aunt Nora clean up the kitchen. Paul is already marking student essays at the table, while both David and Sarah are doing their homework in their rooms. Aunt Nora stacks dishes and runs water into the sink. She has a curious expression on her face

"You know," she says slowly, "it was a funny thing. When I took Beth and Charles down for Beth's appointment, Charles seemed like a different person. He talked endlessly, and he even had colour in his face for a change." Aunt Nora looks at Josselyn, frowning slightly. "And you know what else?"

Josselyn waits.

"I walked them into the office because I had something to do down on the Avenue as well, and once we got Beth inside, Charles turned to me and said that he felt that they had both imposed on Paul and me long enough, and he was going to find a place where he and Beth could stay while he found a job."

"Charles find a job?" Paul had come into the kitchen. He reaches to the cupboard for a coffee mug. "That would be a switch."

Aunt Nora frowns slightly. "Yes," she says. "But it was how he looked. He was so animated—transformed, I would almost say." She looks at Josselyn. "Did anything happen here this afternoon after you came home?"

Josselyn shakes her head. "No. Beth was already up and in the shower when I came home, and I think Charles must have been getting dressed." Josselyn is conscious of the lie as she speaks it.

Aunt Nora considers for a moment but says nothing. Paul, looking noticeably more cheerful, pours himself a cup of decaf, organic coffee. "Good for him," he says. "It's about time he did something for himself."

"I suppose," murmurs Aunt Nora, but she continues to look thoughtful while Josselyn and Paul exchange a glance—would-be conspirators while Aunt Nora muses.

Josselyn says nothing, but opens a drawer and pulls out a dish towel. She glances at the window, feeling a strange intensity of spirit. In a funny way, she feels as though she has scored a point against Aunt Nora and her matronly determination to guide and control all of the events of the household. She feels amused, triumphant, and ashamed all at once.

Aunt Nora suddenly looks at the clock. "Speaking of Beth and Charles—I have to go pick them up, so I'll have to leave the dishes with you." She hurries out of the kitchen.

The front door bangs, and Josselyn leaves the dishes to soak, stepping to the window and staring into the falling snow. The house is quiet, with only the occasional sigh coming from Paul at the dining room table. Josselyn rests her cheek against the glass and watches the snow swirl against the pane. It's dark now and the air so thick that Josselyn can hardly see to the end of the yard. She thinks of the tracks she made in the snow coming home, and how they would be already erased. She thinks of the farm, too, of how the snow would settle over the wide space of ground between the house and the outbuildings; of how it would make little columns on the tops of fence posts, form thick second coats on the backs of the cattle, and fill up the furrows to turn the fields into an even stretch of whiteness. It would fall and fall, and in the morning the world would be changed, made poignant and new by the touch of the transforming snow.

TRACKS

It's weird for me. Sighted people generally want to help. This doesn't mean they're not going to ask a bunch of stupid questions, but if you understand their need to help, then it's a lot easier. You'd be surprised how personal some of this gets. I figure answering the stupid questions is payment for the help. Here are some sample questions.

Most popular sample question: Have you been blind all of your life?

I mostly tell the truth in response to this one, but I don't like to. I got in a car accident when I was a kid. That's usually about all I say. I did tell a guy once that I had battery acid thrown in my face when I was nine. He was good and horrified, but I don't think I gave that as an answer again.

Second most popular question: How do you get around?

Since I get asked this question when I'm out and about anyway, I always wonder why the hell people ask it. I'm walking around right now, aren't I? I don't say this, but I think it. I explain that I take the bus and train, just like regular people.

Third most popular question: What is it like to be blind?

I don't know. What is it like to be stupid? How the hell am I supposed to answer something like that? I usually say it's okay, but I never say very much.

Just so you know, and just so I get it out of the way, I live at my mom's. She works at the post office in the mall, and she collects alimony payments from my loser father. I have an older brother who lives at home, too, but he's an idiot and is hardly ever around, unless he's hungover.

Today, I'm heading downtown on the bus. I like to sit behind the driver on the jump seat. Bus drivers always tell me to sit across the aisle beside the door so they can see me. But I don't like that seat, and I always try to sit behind the driver. It usually annoys the hell out of them. If someone is sitting in my spot, they usually get up and move, especially if I stand there for a moment. They're probably afraid I'm going to sit in their lap.

There I am, heading downtown, and this sincere old lady is sitting beside me. She is going on about how I'm so wonderful because I'm brave enough to go on the bus by myself. I let her talk. I tell her that I'm looking for work at the moment, which is bullshit, but it makes me sound as though I'm doing something with my life. You can never overdo this kind of thing. People want to hear how tough it is for the blind guy to make his way in the world. That way, they can tell me how brave I am, which no doubt helps them to feel better about themselves.

I'm heading downtown to see Harlequin. Harlequin isn't his real name, of course. I think it's Al. Whatever. I'm going downtown to see Harlequin because he's generally out on the square this time of day. Seeing Harlequin can be a pain in the ass, but it beats sitting in my mom's basement.

Harlequin calls himself a street performer, which is crap. He isn't really much better than a panhandler. He has a place downtown somewhere, one of those tiny rooms with hardly anything in it except a bed and a dresser, and the bathroom down the hall. The whole place smells like you wouldn't believe. I went there once. Harlequin took me to his place after he made a good haul on the square. He said we should go back to his place for a toke.

I knew what back to his place was about, and I wasn't interested. I had enough of that sort of shit at the blind school.

But I did want the toke, so I went with him anyway. As it turned out, he didn't have any weed—the asshole. So we drank beer. He had some tequila, too. He taught me how to drink it with salt and lemon, which was all right. I got out of there after a couple of hours.

The bus driver tells me that my stop is next, and I shake off the old lady, although not before she tries to give me a dollar. I figure what the hell and take the dollar. She probably makes more on her pension than I do on AISH, which is the Social Services check that the government gives us handicapped freaks who can't work.

I get off the bus. I'm only a block from the square, so I begin to make my way down the street, using my cane diagonal style.

You probably don't know this, but there are a couple of different ways to use a white cane. You can tap your way down the street, waving your cane from side to side—most likely clipping people as they pass—or you can hold your cane on the angle in front of you, not tapping as you go. I do a combination of both, but it always depends on where I am and where I'm trying to get to. Waving my cane around gets people to look. I suppose they look anyway, but making a show of it usually gives people the chance to get out of the way. Covering myself on-the-angle, as my old mobility instructor at the blind school used to say, is not always as good, but I can move quicker. The only problem here is that I get my cane tangled up in people's legs. Women, especially, don't like it when I get my cane between their legs. Can't say I really blame them.

I make my way down the street, past the city center mall, and cross the street to the square. Harlequin usually sets up across from the library. He makes so much friggin' noise that it's never hard to find him. Today, he's whaling away on his tin whistle, and he stops as I walk up.

"Robbie, my man." He steps forward to give me a cuff on the shoulder. "How's today?"

"All right," I say. I lean on my cane and let my eyes sort of wander off vaguely. This is a thing I do that always sets people a little on edge. At the blind school, they always told us to point our noses at people when we talked to them. I understand about eye contact because I could see until I was nine, but playing up the blind routine is one way of keeping people uneasy. Harlequin isn't fooled. He's seen me do this too often.

"Come on, man," he says. "What are you up to? You looking for some action?"

"Maybe," I say. I didn't have enough money to buy anything from Harlequin, but I wasn't about to tell him that.

Harlequin is a dealer, in a small-time sort of way. It's mostly just pot, but sometimes he'll have other stuff as well. I usually can't afford anything other than the occasional joint.

"Well," he says, "you just let me know, and I'll fix you up, eh."

I nod my head, still letting my eyes wander.

"But hey, how about you give me a hand for a bit? There's probably some beer money in it for you."

Helping Harlequin is pretty simple. It mostly involves me standing there looking very visible to passersby. The idea is that people are more likely to drop change into his hat if he has me standing with him. He calls it the pity factor. People think that Harlequin is a good guy because he's giving the poor blind guy a chance to help him out. I stand there and play the tambourine—or whatever else Harlequin is packing that day—looking pathetic and not very good.

The funny part is I do know something about music, and I can play all kinds of instruments. The blind school was good for that. One time, Harlequin had me play the mandolin while he played the tin whistle. It was fun. We both whaled away for about half an hour. The surprising thing was that he actually got less in coin that day.

Harlequin was pissed off. "If you're going to help me out," he said, "then make people want to give—not walk away."

The asshole.

I stand there, looking as pathetic as I can, and acting like I can't really play the rattle Harlequin handed me. Harlequin plays a ukulele and draws a crowd. He's actually all right once he gets going—good enough to fool the afternoon crowd on the square, anyhow. In half an hour, he has a hat full of change.

"Good enough," he says, and puts his things into his backpack. "All right, buddy, let's take a walk." I latch on to Harlequin's arm and we head off across the square.

Here's where it gets tedious. Harlequin is one of those guys who has an opinion about everything—and I mean everything. He has opinions about the government; he has opinions about movies; he has opinions about parking downtown; he has opinions about the friggin' weather. He doesn't just say it's a nice day. He has an opinion about the sort of nice day it is in comparison to other nice days. You should hear him go on about this nuclear winter thing they're talking about.

Today, Harlequin has an opinion about me. I really hate that. He's going on about some sort of computer for blind people. He says I could get one of these computers and then a job—maybe in a government office, or maybe as a computer programmer.

"You got to go to school for that," I say. "I don't know anything about computers, for Christ's sake. And I'm not going back to school."

"Education, Robbie," he says. "You're a young guy. You got to get educated. Me—I didn't even finish grade nine. But I got some talent, see. So I use my talent to make a living."

Harlequin's got talent, all right. He's got enough talent to use a blind guy to help him collect a hat full of change on the square.

"But you, you're a smart guy, Robbie. Me, I just know stuff, more stuff than lots of people. But you, you got brains."

He's in full flow now.

"So what the hell's the difference?" I ask.

"Lots of difference. Me—I can remember stuff. I remember everything I read. I figure I got one of them photographic-type memories. But you. You got something else."

"And what's that?"

"Robbie," he says, "you got brains and you got potential. More potential than I ever had. You could do something with your life. You could do whatever you wanted! You just got to find your path.

"Take one of those special computers I was telling you about. You get yourself one of them computers, you get yourself a job, and then you come down here and take old Harlequin out for a beer or something." He laughs.

That's just great.

"And how exactly am I supposed to get ahold of one of these special computers? Jesus fucking Christ, Harlequin. Nobody's going to hire a blind guy for anything. I spent six years in a residential school, I came back to finish high school, and now I live on friggin' Social Services. How's that going to look on a résumé?"

I am really starting to get bugged. I can hear it in my voice, and Harlequin can probably hear it, too. I can feel myself beginning to vibrate around the edges, which is never a good sign.

I guess Harlequin is getting the message. He finally shuts up and we cross the street to City Hall where Harlequin finds a bench. We sit down. He counts out his haul and opens my hand to pour in a fist full of coin.

I close my hand around the change. I suddenly feel weird. I want to chuck that handful of change in Harlequin's face, or better yet out over the street. That would make him crazier. He's a little miser, that's what he is—a sly little bloodsucking miser who barely has enough talent to put two notes together. A small-time dealer who likes to fuck little boys.

"What's up, Robbie? You look pissed off."

"No," I say. "I just remembered something that I was supposed to do today."

"You got time for a coffee before you take off?"

"Not really."

"That's cool," he says. "I'm grabbing a coffee and then I've got to see somebody."

I know what that means. He needs to do a deal, see a homeless teenager, or maybe he was bootlegging for some of the old drunks or wandering nutcases on the strip.

"You want a hand back to the square?"

"Nah, I'll be fine." Not wanting to stick around, I leave Harlequin and head for the train.

I walk back across the square and then down the long stairs to the underground. I still feel really bugged. Maybe it was Harlequin, and maybe not. I didn't exactly know. I made myself not care.

Once underground, you have to walk down this long hallway to get to the train. I like it down here. You go up in a series of ramps, and then you get to the top, and then you head down the other side, a ramp at a time.

I get down to the train platform. It's quiet at the moment—still middle of the afternoon. I walk up and down, reaching out with my cane every now and then to find the edge of the platform. I figure people are looking. People always think I'm going to fall off the edge or something.

Whenever I'm standing and waiting for a bus or the train, I do this thing where I roll my cane in my hand and flip it from one hand to the other. The first time Harlequin saw me do this, he said I could have been a juggler if I could see.

I'm flipping my cane from hand to hand, walking a bit back and forth, and then—goddamn it—my cane flips right out of my hand and goes over the edge of the platform. I stand there for a moment, half-frozen in surprise.

Now, if you can see, then you aren't really going to understand what this is like. Maybe you can. Imagine somebody puts you in a dark room. You know there's a hole nearby, but you aren't exactly sure where it is. Think of that guy in that story by Edgar Allan Poe.

But I did know where the edge of the platform was; my friggin' cane just went over it. I stand there for a second, no cane, and wonder what the hell I'm going to do. It pisses me off thinking about my cane down there. I want it back.

Nothing else to do. I get down on the floor and scoot to the edge of the platform. I shimmy around, and then over the edge I go.

It's a longer way down than you might think to those tracks. I'm not especially tall, and the edge of the platform is almost level with my shoulder, that is before I duck down and start feeling around for my cane.

It's sort of cool being down there, but it's a little scary at the same time. I want to find my cane quickly and then get the hell back onto the platform, but I can't find it. What if it bounced or rolled across the tracks? It should be right here where it slipped out of my hand. I feel around in the rocks and then past the nearest rail. Jesus, they're bigger than I thought they would be. I press my palm to the cold metal, getting a sense of its hardness and coldness.

And then I feel something, or maybe I hear something. Anyway, it comes to me like a vibration through the rails, and for one second I wonder what it is. Then I hear the intercom announcing the southbound train. And at the same time, all hell breaks loose.

The whole thing is kind of funny to think about now, but I felt sick about it right afterward, which is weird because stuff like this doesn't usually bother me.

I had to explain to the security guys what I was doing on the tracks. They called in some manager guy of transit, and he gave me supreme shit for going down onto the tracks at all. I practically started bawling over losing my cane until he backed off a little. But that wasn't the part that got to me. It was after the signal sounded for the train, and I realized that I should get the hell out of there.

I hear the announcement, and I still can't find my cane. You remember I said that the platform is almost as high as my shoulder? You try pulling yourself out of a pit when you haven't got any kind of purchase and there's a friggin' train coming.

Nobody must have seen me go over the edge to begin with, but they see me now, head and shoulders over the edge of the platform, with the sound of the approaching train growing to a roar, just like an airplane when it's taking off.

Somebody screams, of course. But that isn't much help. Somebody else begins to run, but I figure I have about three seconds before the train pulls in to the platform and turns me into roadkill.

With my body pressing against the wall of the platform, I can feel with my legs that the platform is undercut or something. My feet and knees slide underneath, even as I try to pull myself out. So I do the thing that makes most sense to me at the time. I drop like a rock and roll right into the crawl space or whatever it is under the platform.

Even from down below, I can hear the screaming as the train pulls in. It seems a whole lot bigger as I curl up in that crawl space, listening to the creaking and clanking of its underside, like it was some great mechanical monster. I hope my cane didn't get run over.

Well, you can imagine how the rest of that went. People shout and scream. I crawl forward until I'm past the front of the train, and then I pop my head up over the edge of the platform. More screaming. Somebody hauls me onto the platform, and I'm brought to the driver who has now come out of the train. The two security guys arrive quickly after that, and I start wailing about my cane right away. I'm thinking that if the crowd is on my side, the security guys would be less likely to arrest me.

Somebody finds my cane, which had flipped onto the other side of the tracks. The train driver is on his radio, which I can hear because I'm standing by the open door to the control room—or whatever you call it. The security guys settle down the crowd and then I ride with them to the university station where we are met by the big shot from transit. More explanations; more wining on my part. Finally, he lets me go with a warning never to go onto the tracks again, even if I do lose my cane down there.

I don't usually mind this kind of thing. It's fun causing a scene, and then acting the pathetic blind guy. Sometimes it's worth it just to see what happens. But this time was different. I don't know that my life was really in danger. I'm sure the driver would have spotted me in time, or the running person would have pulled me up if I hadn't thought of ducking down. But I don't even know if that's it.

I leave the university station and catch a bus down to the Avenue. I like it here better than downtown. I walk along to where I know some panhandlers hang out, and when I figure out where one of them is, I take that whole load of change that Harlequin had poured into my hand and I dump it into his.

"Thanks, man! God bless," he says. He sounds surprised.

"Don't mention it," I say. And I walk off down the street.

As I walk away, I can feel the whole afternoon lodging itself into my brain. I feel sort of sick, and I don't like it, but I don't want to think about it, either. Perhaps if I can ignore it long enough, it will go away. But maybe if I keep telling myself it's just another funny story, it will be all right.

TIFF

It is the sight of my father cradling the body of my cousin that I remember most vividly. I am standing in the front door of the cabin, and I am looking up to see him walking toward me down the steep slope of the drive. The first thing to register is not my cousin, lying heavy in his arms, but that he might slip on the thick, sliding clay beneath his feet.

My cousin is three years older than me. As my father approaches, I can see the soft fall of her hair over her face. She looks asleep. It is a mercy that I can't see where the gunshot has torn away part of the left side of her head. It isn't until much later when I see the bloody smear on my father's coat that I know Tiff is dead.

Tiff was sixteen that summer, and I had become more and more fascinated with Tiff and her older sister, Carol, since I first became aware of girls. My fascination and the events of that morning in July became uneasily mixed in my thirteen-year-old memory: the screaming and crying that follows my father's arrival at the cabin, the later sound of voices in muttered prayer and wailing anguish, and the overarching silence that hangs thickly over the tiny farm for the next two weeks.

"Tiff is a slut." This from Carol, the older of my two cousins. She is talking to me. The three of us are sitting on the low roof of one of the old outbuildings in the yard of the farm. The ground rises steeply away from the cabin, and in the far corner of the building where we sit, the roof is only waist high. We are all reading. Tiff looks up from her book to glare at her sister. Carol is more than a year older than Tiff. I hold my breath.

"He probably doesn't even know what a slut is," says Tiff, looking at me.

"I do," I say. I am clutching my book in my hands. It feels foreign somehow, or maybe it is my hands that no longer feel entirely connected to my body.

"I'm not really a slut," says Tiff. "I just like to fuck."

Carol snorts with laughter, not looking up from her book. "And what," she says, "is the difference?"

Tiff thinks about this for a moment. "I'm not a whore," she says slowly. "Not like that little Kenderley witch. She'll fuck anyone who asks her. I don't do that."

Carol snorts into her book once again. "I still don't get the difference."

Later that afternoon, Tiff and I stand in the midst of the clump of poplars that forms one corner of the farmyard. No one can see us from the house. Tiff has stripped off her T-shirt and is staring down at me.

"You need to be educated," she says. Her skin is sleek and golden, her breasts small, with dark pink nipples. None of this registers until much later. My heart hammers in my chest. She is slightly taller than me and is standing so close that I can smell the scent of cut hay that must come from her hair.

Very slowly, I reach out a hand and press it to her breast. My throat has constricted; it hurts as I try to swallow. I don't know if some sound escapes my throat, but Tiff pulls away. She doesn't look at me until she picks up her T-shirt and pulls it back on over her head. Then she looks at me again.

"Do you know how to kiss?" She is businesslike. I shake my head. I receive my first lesson on kissing from Tiff in that clump of poplars. I am awkward and half-scared out of my mind. But Tiff is patient. When she tells me to stop, she looks down at me with an expression that doesn't fit what we've just been doing. Only much later do I identify this expression as one of kindness, a gentleness with which I am unfamiliar, especially from Tiff. We walk back to the cabin together, and all of my efforts are put into not crying.

"You should read more," Tiff says.

"Like what?" I croak.

"Stuff that will educate you." She gives me a sly sideways glance. "Not just about girls or kissing."

Back in the cabin, Tiff drags me over to her bed. It's a one-room cabin, with partitions dividing things into semiprivate spaces, so it's not really even a bedroom.

Tiff fishes through a pile of books in an old crate. "Here," she says, reaching out a book toward me.

I take it. It's a slender volume, and the title reads, *Gerard Manley Hopkins: Selected Poems*.

I look up. "I don't really read poetry," I mumble.

"Which is why you should read it," she says, in the tone that always makes me feel stupid and inferior.

I say I will read it, but I'm more interested in the pile of clothes on her bed, and the pink underwear that threatens to slide onto the floor. And then we are interrupted by a shout from Mary, Tiff's mother, and we have to go and help with dinner.

Tiff disappears after dinner. They start searching for her at around five o'clock the next morning, not because her parents are shocked to realize she has been out all night, but because a neighbour kid has come banging on the cabin door to tell my aunt and uncle that he thinks Tiff is in trouble. Later, I am told that it was an accident. Tiff was drinking in a neighbour's barn with two boys, and one of them had the rifle. I can never get any more information from my mother about what happened then.

My dad is not able to stay. He has to get back to the city to go to work. I stay with my mother at the farm until after the funeral. I don't remember much of that ten days. It's a blur of people coming and going from the cabin, of food on the table, of strangers with grief-stricken faces. The funeral is held at the Catholic church in town. I've never been to a funeral, let alone a Catholic church, and I find myself staring at the crucified Christ hanging at the front of the church—more violence and death I don't understand.

Before we leave the farm, I find myself again in the little clump of poplars, the place of my first kiss. It is quiet, save for the buzzing of flies and the faraway sounds of a crow. I am back here, I think, to satisfy my own need to grieve. I have seen my own father cry in this last week, but my tears will not come. The last time I felt my eyes burn with tears was in this spot, after feeling Tiff's warm, open mouth. I feel as though I should cry and wonder why I can't. Tiff was my cousin—part of my family—and now she is dead.

We leave at the end of the month. I sit in the backseat of the car and stare numbly out the window, watching telephone poles flip past. The book of poetry is stuffed deep inside my bag.

It takes time for me to push the memory of my father carrying Tiff down the sloping drive on that July morning to the outer edges of my awareness. Two summers after Tiff is killed, I realize one day with a shock that I hadn't thought of her for a long time. The memory of Tiff comes back forcibly one afternoon when my aunt Mary comes for a visit. There she is, sitting at the kitchen table, drinking coffee with my mom. I come in the back door of the house from playing baseball at the nearby school, and stand momentarily shocked to see my aunt. She makes a fuss over me, hugging me, commenting on how tall I am, and pushing the hair back from my forehead to peer into my face. I have refused all summer to let my mother cut my hair. My mother watches from her seat at the table.

Things have changed for my aunt. She and Uncle Rob have separated. The farm was sold earlier that year, and Carol has moved to Toronto. My aunt, it appears, is moving to Calgary. She has accepted a job in a library at a university. This is what my aunt did before she and Uncle Rob bought the farm, before she became the woman who dressed in jeans, jack shirts, and oversize rubber boots, and who spent every morning clomping her way around the yard to feed chickens and pigs.

I have to glean the information from their conversation. Adults generally don't like to tell kids anything, while acting as though you have been part of the conversation all along. This means I have to piece the bits together in order to get a picture. I don't ask about Carol, and I don't say anything about Tiff.

After that summer, I drift as a teenager. I never have a girlfriend, but I do get a job, a lousy job bagging groceries and stocking shelves at the Safeway down the street. But I'm able to save some money, and by the time I finished high school, it looked as though I was on my way to having a life of my own.

The summer I'm nineteen, I lose my footing on a slope of shale in Jasper during a hike with two friends. I fall thirty meters, and no one knows why I wasn't killed. I suffer a head injury, a broken leg, and five fractured ribs, which keeps me in the hospital for three months. It is a foggy time for me, muffled and blurry. My vision has been affected, and I can't bring anything into focus. I take another year to recover. By that time my world has changed so much that looking back before the fall I can hardly recognize that person as me. It is as though my fall has laid down an impenetrable barrier between me and my earlier life. It is around this time, too, that my father moves out of the house, and the split with my earlier life is irreparable.

When I am fully recovered, I go to university. I meet women, which is both a revelation and a source of vague unease. Three relationships follow, all of which fail, and I have part of an evening with a woman whom I do not know. I go to grad school, and I meet Cynthia, and it finally looks as though I'm getting the life I think I'm supposed to have. We get married and have a daughter, Sidney. Cynthia, my wife, decides to leave when Sidney is twelve. The fog returns, and things are blurry once again, and my past superimposes itself on my present. It is as though Cynthia's leaving has reactivated the memories of my accident, and I can't stop myself from falling into them at unexpected times. I am a young man again, broken and bleeding and unable to move. I am in the hospital again, confined to a bed, trying to bring my world into focus. I remember a lot of drinking, but eventually I wake up to my situation, and to my daughter who desperately needs a parent, and I manage to pull myself together.

Sidney is now nineteen. She is in her second year of university, and she has a social life that I find staggering. She brings home her girlfriends, who are sometimes more women than girls.

One such friend is Courtney. Sid and Courtney arrive at the house one afternoon at the beginning of October while I am sitting in the living room marking essays from one of my classes at the college where I teach.

I watch the two of them getting out of Sid's car. They are young, healthy, and beautiful. I walk into the kitchen to see if there's something I can offer them. This is what I do—the bachelor dad who doesn't drink anymore, who teaches university English and looks after the house, and who keeps track of his ebullient daughter. They are coming into the house while I rummage the cupboards for snacks.

"Hey," says Courtney, coming up the stairs and into the kitchen.

I look at her, not directly, and say something that is meant to make her laugh. She does, and I am gratified. Courtney is one of the few who has never been bothered by how I have to look at people. Because of my head injury, and something to do with the optic center of my brain, anything that I look at straight on and from too close a distance goes out of focus. I have to look slightly to the right or left in order to properly see what I'm looking at. Most people find this disconcerting. The classroom is fine because I can always keep my students at a distance.

The two of them sit down at the table. They unabashedly eat chocolate chip cookies, gulping down milk and laughing until they are wiping tears from their eyes. Tonight, they are going dancing.

"And then to Steph's house," says Sid.

I have to think. Steph is all right. "Whose car are you taking?" I ask.

"I'm driving tonight," says Courtney. "Sid always drives, so it's my turn."

There is one awkward moment for me before they go out for the evening. I am heading down the stairs to my study. Sidney is in the bathroom, but I almost run into Courtney at the bottom of the stairs. I can't see anything when I first move from light to shadow, which Courtney knows, so she brushes off my apology. For a moment I am aware of her.

Her figure comes swimming into my field of vision. She is looking at me curiously. She has a woman's body, full breasted and full hipped, large green eyes, a wide, sensual mouth, and dark hair cut around an oval face that I have seen alternately serious and full of mischief.

"I'm sorry, Courtney," I say awkwardly. "I'm blind as a bat when I first come down here." She laughs, and allows me to pass into my study.

Sid and Courtney leave shortly after, but I continue to be unsettled. Something in that basement encounter has me feeling uneasy. I don't know why. I'm used to being around young, attractive women who are full of energy. Most of Sidney's friends fall into that category. And in some measure they are still girls. I remember many of them as kids: skinny, shrill, or just loud, some with glasses or braces.

The college where I teach is full of these girls/women. They come in every variety: some younger, some older, some nervous and quiet, some loud and abrasive; some are studious, some are on display, many are bored. For the time they are sitting in my classes I have their attention, or I get it when I ask them to put away their phones. But they are all young, and I keep them where I can see them.

Later, I fall asleep on the couch and wake with a gasp when my phone rings. I don't know the time.

"Hi, is this Sidney's dad?"

I don't know the voice.

"Yes," I say. "Who is this?" I struggle to become aware of where and when I am.

"Sidney's not doing so well. She needs help."

"Who is this?" I say again. I can feel the panic rising in my throat. "Who are you? Where are you?"

"Sidney's passed out. I think you should come and get her."

I manage to get an address, and then I call a cab. Because of my head injury, I do not drive. I pace up and down in front of the house watching for headlights. It is after two o'clock in the morning. What the fuck has happened? Where is my child?

The cab finally arrives, and I give him the address. I feel sick with apprehension. I press the button to lower the window in case I need to vomit. My brain is screaming, but as usual at a time like this, my body becomes paralyzed. I am unable to think clearly, and I am forcing my limbs to move, as though my body is that of a leaden marionette.

We finally arrive at an apartment block. There are people on the lawn. I walk up the sidewalk, moving my feet automatically, and I can see Sidney walking down the steps of the apartment toward me. She catches sight of me right away.

I cannot feel relief yet. There is too much of me that has been split off in order to be here. "Are you all right?" I ask.

She nods. She is crying and trying to hide it. I wait until we get home to ask. Yes, she was drinking more than she should have. And no, she didn't pass out. She doesn't know who called.

"And what happened to Courtney?" I ask. "I thought she was the one who was going to be the driver. I thought she was going to watch out for you?" I want to blame Courtney. I want to blame somebody. My relief gives way to the fear I couldn't feel in the cab, and my ever-present sense of guilt doesn't allow me to be fair.

"Courtney had a phone call," says Sidney. "She left just after we got to Steph's."

Not able to stop myself, I say, "Do you know what happens to girls who pass out at parties?"

"Dad, I was fine. I didn't pass out."

We are standing in the kitchen. I am agitated, which means that I have trouble forming words. "I thought you were hurt," I finally manage.

But Sid is unrelenting. She stands opposite the table from me. She is small-boned, like her mother. Her fine, dark-blond hair is coming loose, and she pushes it back impatiently. Her face has a dogged expression. "I was fine, Dad. I'm not twelve. I'm not a little girl anymore. And I'm not a stupid sixteen-year-old who's going to get herself in trouble at a party. I'm turning twenty next month."

Something in her voice or manner penetrates my agitation. I sit down hard on a kitchen chair and rub my face with my hands. "All right," I say. "I'm sorry."

I don't talk to Sidney much in the next couple of days. My feelings seem disproportionate to the situation, but I'm not able to see them clearly. Not knowing what to do with the way I am feeling, I wash walls, vacuum, and go through shelves and boxes that I haven't touched in months.

On the Sunday, I find boxes at the back of a shelf beneath the back stairs, boxes that have followed me for years, moving in my wake as I moved from place to place, and always finding a home in an out-of-the-way spot. I open them one at a time. The book that I find is small, the cover blurred and edges limp. I open to the flyleaf. In faded ink is written:

For Tiff
Happy Birthday.

It is a collection of poems by Gerard Manley Hopkins. I don't know who has given the book to Tiff. I let the book fall open to a poem. It is "Pied Beauty."

I clutch the book in my hands, kneeling there on the cold concrete of the basement floor, and I remember Tiff, my cousin Tiff, with her warm brown eyes, smooth golden skin, and slightly too-thin frame. Her image comes to me forcibly across the gap of years. This is Tiff, my cousin Tiff—contrary and capricious, generous and kind, looking at me out of warm brown eyes, and asking me if I know how to kiss.

Glory be to God for dappled things.

Tiff has underlined the words. What did she see in this poem? How did my often sarcastic and irreverent cousin understand God's glory? And what did God's glory have to do with the corpse I remember, inert and childlike, laid out in a coffin at the front of a church?

The loss that I was never able to feel then, and the loss that I am somehow always expecting now, comes rolling toward me like a wave, and it catches me there as I kneel on the cold concrete of the basement floor. I am glad Sidney isn't home.

It is as though I have broken through a wall to discover feelings I have forgotten, feelings of a younger self, an unfamiliar self, who was in love with his cousin, and who followed her around in the hopes of a glance, a kind word, or anything that will tell me she has taken notice.

And I see my father again, moving now as he comes toward the house carrying the body of my cousin, and I am backing up as he steps over the threshold while my aunt cries out in anguish.

THE END OF SUMMER

Sammy wanted her to sell the house. She supposed it wasn't so much having to leave the house anymore, or even that he thought she should move into the Kiwanis lodge in Edmonton; it was that at some level she had known for months that this was coming, and she had done nothing to prepare herself for a decision that was no longer hers.

The week before, Sammy had come to the house in the middle of the afternoon, a thing he rarely did. He had stood by the back steps, absently scuffing a boot against the sidewalk and looking off into the middle distance, while he talked vaguely about the transmission in the old John Deere being shot and this year's canola crop not being any better than last's. Melvina simply waited. She knew her son well enough to know that he didn't come to talk to her about crops. Finally, he looked at her and said if she didn't talk to the Realtor in the next week, then he would do it himself. Melvina hadn't looked up from the basket of pansies she was repotting, but she told him that if she were ever going to sell the house, she would do it in her own goddamn time. That made him flinch. He never liked it when she swore, but she needed him to know that the house was hers, and she wasn't about to be pushed into selling before she was ready.

Part of her had been ready all this past year, but Melvina wasn't about to tell him that. She couldn't argue with the fact that it had become more difficult for her to keep up the little house and even harder for her to work in the garden. Harve hadn't helped much in the five years they had lived in town, but he had been of some use. Lately, there were some days when her hands became as stiff as claws and it was all she could do to even wash the dishes.

Setting down another of the potted geraniums on the edge of the porch to keep it out of the afternoon sun, Melvina straightened, feeling the ache in her back and legs. It hadn't rained for over a month. The air was hot and stifling, wrapping up the town as if in a wool blanket. She wasn't angry with Sammy, not really. She felt only a kind of regret, dry and brittle, like her garden that despite her best efforts was withering in the August heat.

Melvina and her husband had lived in the little house in town ever since harve had given over the farm to Sam. It was only Melvina herself who still called him Sammy, mostly to remind him that she was his mother and that once upon a time he had been a child. When Harve had died last year, Melvina knew that she would eventually have to make a decision about where she would live, all the while ignoring the nagging sense that the choice was being made for her.

harve had been admitted to the hospital in Edmonton with prostate cancer just before Christmas. Melvina had stayed with her grandson Gordon and his new wife, Louise, all through January and February, and she had gone up to the hospital nearly every afternoon to sit with Harve. Sitting with him had been all she could do. Her husband had always been a quiet man, shy and withdrawn, saying little to anyone, even Melvina. In the hospital he had said less, withdrawing so completely that he only spoke as a means of having his needs met—water, food, the bedpan.

Melvina sat, reading to him from detective novels or the *Reader's Digest*, and watched his gaunt form shrivel away to nothing. He seemed to be dying by degrees. His skin, the colour of wet concrete, hung in folds over his bones. Looking at him reminded Melvina of winters on the farm when she used to drape the sheets over the old drying rack in the basement. He was like that, all lines and sharp angles, skin hung over bones like laundry over a wooden frame. But despite his emaciated body, his eyes had stayed the same: a pale, remote blue, like the sky on a summer's afternoon. They were eyes used to looking across wide-open spaces, over field after field of standing grain to the hazy edge of earth and sky. She often wondered if he had ever really seen anything up close, if he had ever really seen her.

Harve died on an afternoon in March, one of those early spring days when winter tries to reassert itself, freezing slush into ridges and points of ice that made walking impossible. After the funeral Melvina had felt only relief—relief at not having to sit in that hospital room any longer, and relief at not having to watch his weathered face set in lines that bespoke an unutterable conviction and an absolute denial.

It was only later, as winter passed into spring, that Melvina began to resent her husband. She couldn't understand the feeling, but she felt cheated, made a fool of, just as though all the years on the farm counted for nothing now that Harve was dead. Maybe it had been in the way that Sammy had looked at her after the funeral. All those years of keeping the house, of cooking for five, of getting the children out in time to meet the school bus, of helping harve in the fields, of waiting for the rain to come or the rain to stop, forever walking a line between the weather on one hand and the bank on the other, were nothing to Sammy. She had been a farm wife, and now she wasn't even that, just an old woman with a foul mouth, who stubbornly refused to admit she could no longer look after her own house.

Melvina refilled the watering jug from the hose and began to make her painstaking round of the garden. She carefully watered each plant as she went. She had made her way past the lilies and the hollyhocks to the roses when she noticed a bee buzzing around one of the pink roses that hung limply in the heat. It didn't light, but circled the rose with a clumsy sort of grace that seemed to draw a quivering response from the flower.

Melvina watched the bee. She hadn't seen a bee for what seemed weeks. It had been so hot and dry through most of July and all of August that perhaps that had kept them away, and maybe she just hadn't noticed.

The bee continued its circling, and the heat pressed down. The silence seemed to gather in and fill the garden, an expectant pause like a drawn breath, the only sound being the buzzing of the bee. Melvina watched it while the silence drew itself out and out. She felt herself carried away by that silence to a place both long ago and far away, a place without walls, without words. She closed her eyes. She saw a graceful swirl of colour that formed itself into the exquisite picture of another garden: masses of flowers—fiery orange, deepest red, and palest yellow—and a rag doll with brown woolen hair and an ivory dress.

Melvina opened her eyes. With an odd feeling of surprise, she found that she was still in her own backyard. Everything looked the same, but it was odd, somehow, as though she were seeing it from the wrong angle. She felt herself struggling, groping after something before she had a chance to know that it was even there.

Melvina set down the watering jug and walked slowly back into the house. She sat through the rest of the morning, the silence still pressing close all around her.

It was the jangle of the telephone that finally brought Melvina back to herself. She got up stiffly and went into the kitchen.

"Mom. That you, Mom?"

The voice was loud in the receiver. It was Nora, Sammy's wife. Melvina took a slow breath and rolled her eyes. Who in god's name did she think it would be! Nora firmly believed that anyone over the age of eighty-five was either deaf, stupid, or both. She also had a way of talking about Melvina in the third person when other people were around, as though Melvina were one of her grandchildren.

"Yes, Nora. Hello."

"Mom, I talked to Gordon this morning. He and Louise should get here around supper time."

"All right," Melvina said, evenly.

"Okay, Mom." Melvina could hear the indulgent smile in her daughter-in-law's voice. "Gordon said he'd just drop off Louise and Molly and then pop into town to pick you up. Okay, Mom?"

"That's fine, Nora."

"All right, Mom. See you at supper."

Melvina was sitting on the front porch when Gordon pulled up in the old Ford. Gordon was as much unlike Sammy as Sammy was like his own father. He was the only one of her four grandchildren whom Melvina still saw on a regular basis. He was tanned, wearing a T-shirt and cutoffs, with a blue-and-white bandanna tying back his long hair. He looked better than the last time Melvina had seen him, but he still had something of that furtive look about him that had first appeared when he stopped drinking more than two years ago. At the time, he would hardly meet Melvina's eyes, and he seemed constantly in motion, even when he was sitting still. Molly had been only a year and a half old when Gordon came home to the basement suite where he lived with his first wife, to find everything tidy, no sign of Pat, Molly's mother, and Molly herself fast asleep in the daybed.

"Nan!" called Gordon, slamming the car door and walking across the grass. "You look great!"

Gordon always tried hard. He was more like his father than he would ever admit, but sometimes he reminded her of Sammy—her son, blissfully unaware of everyone except himself.

Melvina sighed and gathered up her bag. Gordon met her with a hug, and then he guided her down the stairs and together they walked to the car, Gordon holding the door for her as Melvina climbed stiffly into the front seat. He drove slowly, telling Melvina about how Molly was looking forward to kindergarten and how Louise was still getting used to her new job. The windows were rolled down, but the hot wind did nothing to cool Melvina's face and neck.

After supper that evening, Melvina sat at the kitchen table with Molly cutting out paper roses. In the other room, Nora was talking to Gordon and Louise over the blare of the television—and managing to succeed. Melvina could just see Louise from where she sat at the kitchen table, a tall, full-figured young woman with short, sensible blond hair, now wearing a carefully neutral expression on her face.

Melvina cut out tiny roses with a deliberateness that belied her aching hands, while Molly pasted them into wildly coloured bouquets on a sheet of white pasteboard. The table was covered with bits of paper, pencil crayons, wax crayons, and felts. Molly was finishing her third bouquet, a vivid collage of red, yellow, green, and purple roses.

"Nan," said Molly, pasting in an orange rose. "Did you colour when you were little?"

Melvina didn't pause in her careful cutting. She held the paper close so she could see to follow the outlines of the flower.

"Colour," said Melvina. "Not so much. I didn't have crayons and things the way you have now."

"What did you have?" Molly put down her glue stick and looked at Melvina curiously.

"Well, I had a doll, like you have. My mother always had a flower garden. That was far away from here—in a place called Scotland. In the summer I would bring my doll outside and sometimes we would have tea. I would take her around to each flower and introduce her."

"You mean you talked to the flowers?"

"Yes, I suppose. I would bring my doll to the tiger lily and say, Polly, this is the tiger lily. Tiger lily, this is Polly."

"Was Polly your special doll?"

"Yes she was. Polly came with me on a ship all the way across the ocean and then on a train all the way across the country. Sometimes Polly would get scared, for it was such a long way, but I would talk to her and then she wouldn't be so afraid."

"I have a special doll. Her name is Sarah," said Molly. "Sometimes she gets scared, but I talk to her, too."

Melvina began to cut again, and Molly continued with her pasting. Then Molly said, "Nan, will you have a garden when you move away?"

Melvina looked at her. "What do you mean, dear?"

"Grandma said you're going to move to a 'partment in the city, where we live. How come you're not going to stay in your house, Nan?"

"Well, Molly," said Melvina, carefully cutting around the edge of a petal. She had to work to keep her voice even. "It's getting hard for me to look after the house and the garden all by myself. It might be better if I could live in a place where I could get some help." Melvina did not look up from her cutting, but she could feel Molly watching her.

"Nan," Molly said, "if you lived in a 'partment you wouldn't have a garden anymore. It would be like where Daddy and Louise and me live. It's no fun because Daddy won't let me go to the park by myself. Sometimes I just want to go outside, but I can't. So then I just have to sit in my room. I don't like it."

Melvina put down the scissors. She felt again that wave of feeling that had come upon her in the morning, a sense of something lost, out of reach and beyond recall. Molly was staring at her, straight hair framing her face, eyes intent. Melvina wanted to say something, but she had no words. Very slowly, she reached out and gently touched Molly's cheek, brushing back the fall of brown hair.

Gordon drove Melvina home after she had tucked Molly into bed. The air had become so thick Melvina found it hard to breathe. Thunder muttered and rolled, and the whole sky seemed to light up with every flash of lightning, throwing a glare over the road and the fences to either side.

It took Melvina a long time to get to sleep. The storm finally broke in the middle of the night, a downpour of heavy rain that rattled off the roof, and she had to get up and close the windows against the wind and rain that was blowing across the bedroom floor.

Standing now at the kitchen window, Melvina looked out at the falling rain. It misted into fine needles of spray that blew hissing against the window. The clock on the stove read 5:10.

Melvina suddenly remembered she had left the porch window open the day before to let in some air. She shuffled to the glass door and opened it. The linoleum was wet, and there in the exact center of the floor was a dead bee.

She stared at it. Painfully, she knelt and reached out a finger to gently touch the furry body. It was light and lifeless. For a long moment she held still. Then, she got to her feet and went to get her shoes and her raincoat. She returned to the porch to carefully wrap the dead bee in a tissue, and then went out into the rain.

The air seemed full of water. The wind blew it in fine sheets and tossed the branches of the Manitoba maple. Melvina passed the shuddering lilac and walked across the yard to the roses that had been beaten down by the rain into a tangled mass of red and white and yellow. She unwrapped the dead bee and let it fall into the tangle. For a long time, she stood looking down at the ruined flowers, tears burning her eyes that mingled with the fine rain blowing into her face.

And slowly, very slowly, she raised her arms and began to dance. Ponderously, awkwardly, like a great, dark, high-stepping bird she swayed and circled. With her face turned up to the iron sky, she danced. The wind and the rain were carrying the summer away into memory, to join those of other summers, in town and on the farm, long days of hot sun and the smell of dust that repeatedly and relentlessly darkened into winter. And as she danced, she could feel the memories of all those summers, of those months and years running off of her like the rain, sliding away into nothing. Relieved of the years, her limbs grew lighter, and she felt herself alone, a fixed point between heaven and earth, with nothing more to be or to become, while the world spun slowly about her, the rain blurring into gray clouds overhead and the earth moving beneath her feet.

A VISIT TO THE CALGARY ZOO

As soon as the words were out of his mouth, he wanted to take them back. "It's November," said Louise flatly. "And it's already after two. I'd rather not drive after dark."

From where he sat in the backseat of the car, Gordon could see the perceptible hunching of his wife's shoulders, which meant that she was bracing herself for an argument.

But suddenly Gordon didn't care. "It'll be fun," he said, perching himself sideways on the seat to feed Jonathan some applesauce. His son squealed as half a spoonful went onto his chin, and Gordon dabbed at Jonathan's face with a tissue, glancing sideways into the front seat where Louise was driving determinedly, and Molly was slumped in the passenger's seat, oblivious to everything around her.

"It's November," Louise said again.

"Sure," countered Gordon, "but it won't be busy, and the kids will like it. If we stop for an hour, we'll still have an hour of daylight, and I can drive the rest of the way."

"Why do you want this?"

Gordon had to think about that. He wasn't sure if he could explain why he wanted to stop at the zoo, nor would he ever fully admit to the perverse streak of mulishness that was goading him on. "We've never stopped before, and I'd like to," he said, groping for something that sounded close to reasonable. This answer didn't even convince Gordon, and he was already second-guessing himself before he could think of anything else to say.

This is how it usually went on the way home from their twice-yearly trips to Lundbreck Falls. They argued about where they should stop for gas, or whether or not they should stop in Red Deer for coffee and snacks, or who was going to drive and who was going to entertain Jonathan in the backseat. Gordon found that sometimes it was nearly a week before he and Louise were speaking to each other for more than five minutes at a time. Granted, they hadn't before argued about stopping at the zoo, but fundamentally it wasn't different from any of the other arguments.

Trips in the car were somewhat easier now that Jonathan was three and Molly ten, but the visits home to the ranch were always an ordeal for Louise. The stretch from Edmonton to Red Deer was usually okay; past Innisfail Louise began to get tense, and after Olds, she talked less and less, until she said hardly anything at all once they took the exit onto Highway 3 west past Calgary.

Time spent at the ranch was always something of a study in contrasts. Betty's chatty efficiency was a relief from Bill's dour silences, but Betty would grow brighter with talk and offers of food, while Bill went from moodily silent to openly sullen, with Louise growing louder in her attempts to talk around her father. For his part, Bill, a cattle rancher for all of his adult life, who felt himself entirely subject to the caprices of weather and the price of beef, most often broke his own silence to berate everything from the Conservatives to the Alberta Wheat Pool, but Gordon noticed that it was against her father's silences rather than his rants that Louise braced herself every time they visited the ranch.

Gordon tried to like his father-in-law. When he first met Louise, he was gratified to finally meet someone who hadn't grown up in the city. Pat, Molly's mother, had hated the farm where Gordon grew up and what she called his redneck relatives, but with Louise, it seemed to be different. He tried to bring some of that warmth to bear when he and Molly first met Louise's parents. Betty was thrilled when the three of them first came to spend the weekend at the ranch, but Bill simply retreated into himself and hardly spoke the entire time they were there.

Surprisingly, and with each successive visit, Gordon saw that it was Molly who drew the old man out. With inexplicable devotion, she followed him around, demanding nothing while Bill patiently showed her how to do small jobs around the place—changing the spark plug in the truck or mending a section of broken fence. The old man had won Molly's heart, and he knew no other way to reciprocate than by dragging the little girl around the farm while he worked and tinkered. But the fine line of tension between Louise and her father was always there, and visits to the ranch always left Gordon feeling as though it was somehow his fault that Louise didn't get along with her father.

Sitting now in the backseat of the car, Gordon wished again that he had never mentioned the goddamn zoo. Louise took her eyes from the road long enough to turn and give him one look. "Fine," she said, and she was pulling the car over to take the next exit off the Deerfoot and into the city.

It took them the better part of an hour to get across town to the zoo, and by that time, of course, both kids were hungry. It being so late in the year, the concession stands were closed, and Molly complained loudly about getting salt and vinegar chips instead of ketchup from the machine, while Jonathan promptly spilled orange pop all over himself. Luckily, Gordon had another of Jonathan's shirts in his backpack, but there was nothing they could do about the coat except wipe it down with a paper towel.

First they came to the large building that housed the elephants. Outside, the paddock was empty, and the grass already a winter brown; inside, the three elephants moved in ceaseless circles around the cement enclosure. Opposite to the elephants was the giraffe, hooves clattering as it moved around inside its pen, and farther along were the hippos in their wide pool. Molly was sullen and distinctly not impressed, and Jonathan began to cry because Louise told him in a taut voice that, "No, you cannot play in the water."

It wasn't until they entered the building housing the gorilla enclosure that Jonathan began to settle down. Always ready to take advantage of his son's interest, Gordon crouched beside Jonathan and pointed through the thick glass that fronted the enclosure. "Look, Jonathan.

Look at the two smaller ones there in the corner." He pointed to a pair of yearling gorillas, long armed and wrestling on the floor. "And those are the females—the mommies," he corrected himself rather foolishly, pointing this time to a heap of what looked like boulders at the back of the enclosure where three female gorillas sat watching the yearlings. They looked, Gordon thought, for all the world like three grumpy old women sitting on a bus bench.

Jonathan was staring round-eyed into the enclosure, one index finger in the corner of his mouth. "Big monkeys," he said in a half whisper.

"They're not monkeys, Jonathan," said Molly disdainfully. "They're gorillas." She had refused to kneel before the enclosure, and now stood looking at the gorillas with a teenage disdain that belied her ten years.

Gordon sighed and shifted his crouch to look back at Louise, standing against the opposite wall and fidgeting with her keys. She was a tall woman with short blond hair, full hipped and full breasted, with a wide supple mouth, now closed in that expression Gordon recognized as her way of not becoming angry.

These past three days at the ranch had made Gordon realize just how difficult things were becoming at home. It was his idea to stay home full-time with the kids, but it wasn't working out quite the way he expected. Louise wasn't happy working only part-time after Jonathan was born, and when she was offered a position as literary arts consultant, Gordon encouraged her to take it. He had been at home with the kids for over a year now, and he and Molly had been alone for three years before he had met Louise. But lately he'd felt more and more as the outsider, and less and less as though he belonged in his own home.

For one thing, he was having difficulty understanding Molly. She kept him at arm's length, almost literally, and it was as though she were siding against him in some way. Sometimes after school or in the evenings he would ask her if she wanted to read or play a game, or do any of the things they had always done together, and she would refuse, getting that look on her face that always left him feeling baffled and hurt. As for Jonathan, he allowed Gordon to hold him, change him, read to him, feed him, but his real ally was Louise. Lately, when Louise would come home, Gordon felt as though he were being dismissed, like he was the day shift, after which his services were no longer required. Hard as he tried, his children seemed to elude him. He hadn't dared touch his wife in what seemed like weeks, and the longer he avoided her, the more distant she became, and the more she seemed to treat him like a stupid child.

Gordon glanced up now at Molly, and thought he could see a guarded curiosity in her face. One of the females had shambled down from the rocks and had come right up to the front of the enclosure. She picked up a stick and poked it into a glass case about the shape and size of a fish tank. "She's going to try to get some ants," Gordon said in a whisper.

"Dad," said Molly, "you don't have to whisper. It's not like they can hear you, you know."

Gordon forced himself not to react. He looked at Jonathan. His son's eyes seemed to get even rounder as he stared at the gorilla. Methodically, the female dipped the stick into the case and drew it out to carefully lick away the ants.

"An ant-sickle," whispered Gordon. Molly made a heroic effort not to smile, but she was now looking interestedly at the gorilla. Gordon glanced back at Louise again. His wife's face had momentarily softened; she was looking not at the gorilla but at the two children.

Watching his wife watching the children, Gordon felt his heart lurch. He could feel the scene before him taking shape in his mind like a tableau, a memory he knew he could hold. He hung on to it. There had been so few moments like this in the past year that he didn't want to let it go. He closed his eyes and tried to breathe it in, take it into his body, to hold it, contain it, and absorb it.

And then all hell broke loose inside the enclosure. When Gordon looked again, the female was scrambling back to the pile of rocks, and the yearlings were scattering, their howls and cries loud through the thick Plexiglas. And Jonathan was howling as well, screaming bloody murder as he shrank away from the glass and across the hallway to Louise.

"Jonathan. It's okay," said Gordon, scrambling to his feet.

But Jonathan was already up in Louise's arms, making more noise than what was coming from inside the enclosure. "He's frightened," she said. Gordon could see the harassed look on her face, and he braced himself, waiting for her to become angry, to blame him for making them all come here to the zoo when they could have been most of the way home by now.

Louise was rocking Jonathan back and forth, trying to soothe him with the motion of her body, and crooning softly over his blond head. Gordon waited for her to lash out, but she didn't. She wasn't even looking at him. She just rocked and crooned, one cheek pressed to Jonathan's hair, her eyes growing distant, the lines of her face relaxing out of the rigidity that had become like a mask.

With a shock, Gordon realized that Louise wasn't angry, that she wasn't going to get angry, that she wasn't even considering him at all. He suddenly understood that he was at the edge of her sphere of awareness, had been for some time—weeks, possibly months. He could no more draw a response from her than a passing car. He was part of the background of her world, something she only had to deal with peripherally, and when he demanded her attention, he became the whining adult whose needs were more intrusive than those of the children.

Louise turned away. "I'll take him outside," she said. And with that she left the building.

Gordon stood there feeling oddly foolish. Molly was staring at him. She had dropped her teenage facade—looking more like herself—but she was embarrassed, and Gordon knew it was embarrassment for him. "I'll go wait outside, too," she said, and hurried after Louise.

And there he was, left standing in front of the gorilla enclosure, and horribly uncertain of what had just happened. He turned back to the enclosure slowly, not wanting to follow the others and trying to get a grip on whatever it was he was feeling.

There was a second window that opened onto the other half of the enclosure, and Gordon stopped to peer inside. Coming steadily toward him across the floor was the silverback. It was enormous—massive head and swinging arms, black-brown, with a sprinkling of gray down its spine. Gordon was stunned to see how much larger and heavier the male was compared to the three females. The massive head turned and saw him. Gordon had a sudden, shrinking sense that it was only Plexiglas between him and this great ape that looked as though it could come right through the front of the enclosure if it wanted. But the eyes that looked back at him were calm and gentle, despite the frowning browridges, which gave the masklike face a fierce expression.

There was both intelligence and a regard in those eyes. It had settled itself on the floor, and now it was staring up at Gordon, lazily batting at a hanging rope with one foot. The signs posted below the glass said that it was important to kneel down before the glass and not look the animals in the eyes, but the silverback didn't seem to care. He just looked right back, yawning occasionally and scratching, as though he was less interested in Gordon than Gordon was in him.

Gordon leaned against the glass and stared down. He tried to decide what he saw in the eyes. They were dark brown, clear and curious. Their expression was decidedly not human, although there was an alien awareness that held Gordon where he stood. The great ape's shape was human, and that, together with the expression in the eyes, was enough to send a cold prickle down Gordon's back. It wasn't self-awareness he saw, but perhaps its absence was what made Gordon feel cold. This creature took for granted its own power and self-possession: the strength in the massive hands and arms, the incisor teeth that showed whenever it yawned its indolent yawn, and that alien intelligence that looked calmly back at him from the floor.

And it *was* an intelligence. Gordon was certain of that. It was just not one akin to his own, not knowable, not reachable. He remembered hearing that the apes never had direct contact with any of the staff at the zoo, and that they were made to live out their lives inside the walls of their enclosure, but he found that he couldn't muster any outrage on their behalf, no offended sense of righteousness at these creatures forever shut away in their enclosure.

Gordon closed his eyes and pressed his forehead to the heavy glass, willing himself to imagine what it was like from inside: the dank, humid air, the muffled sounds from outside, the bland faces peering in. It was a world entirely separate from what he knew, cut off and alien, recalling something older, both distant and remote from the cement and the glass—a sense not his own. The recollection of a dream of some alien forest, vivid with the green of leaves and heavy with the smell of earth, where figures gathered quietly among the trees, speaking with eye and body, all in the recognition of place in relation to the group, with an ear always tuned to the forest around to ensure the safety of all.

Gordon shuddered away from the glass and opened his eyes. The enclosure before him was empty. Only the rope hanging from the ceiling swung idly back and forth, as though stirred by a gentle breeze. He felt a pang of loss with the disappearance of the ape. Recalling with difficulty where he was, Gordon knew he should hurry and meet Louise and the kids outside, but he felt himself groping after that fleeting sense of the life so different from his own, patiently living out its days within clearly marked boundaries. For the briefest of moments, he had touched something. But even as he reached after it, it was already slipping away, the primitive recognition of something he could not quite grasp.

Gordon exhaled a long breath. He thought of the long drive back to Edmonton, the days and weeks that would follow, of living with Louise, of watching his children grow and change, of playing out his own part that every day meant less and less to him, despite his effort to give those days some meaning. Turning away from the empty enclosure, Gordon hurried toward the exit and pushed his way into the dull gray of the November afternoon, where the first flakes of winter were beginning to drift down through the still, waiting air. Gordon looked for his family. He caught sight of them, their backs brought into relief by the falling snow, Louise's shoulders slightly hunched as she carried Jonathan, and Molly trailing behind in her perpetual slouch. Gordon hurried to catch up.

THE PAPER MAN

I can't say that I understand my depression. It's not as though it's debilitating in any way. Not like Jay, that's for sure, who went half-crazy one night, phoning almost everyone he knew and telling them everything was fine and not to worry, until his mom called the police because she thought he would kill himself. Jay was in the hospital for two weeks before they released him to his parents back in Galahad, armed with enough drugs to impress the hell out of any self-respecting hypochondriac. Before they let him go, they told him he's bipolar, a fact Jay is quite proud of. He told me they gave him a pamphlet that says Hemingway and other famous people—writers, mostly—were bipolar. I'm not sure I believe the part about famous writers, but if it's true, then he's in good company.

As for me, I have to work at getting through the day. People who just go about their lives don't get it. Most days, it's an effort for me to move through my day, like walking into a strong wind. Some days are worse, and some are better, and I'm never sure which it will be.

My last psychologist called this low-grade depression. She told me that I should try to explore my depression, try to discover what feelings are lying beneath it. Talk to it. Make friends with it. Treat it as though it's something separate from myself, like another person. Not a good idea. I already talk to myself, but getting to know myself in such a way seems a little too personal.

My wife, unlike my psychologist, does not approve of depression. Approve is maybe a little strong, but Kathryn is not from Galahad, and she doesn't know what growing up in that town can do to you. I don't really expect her to understand. She's a city girl—cosmopolitan and all that, and very unlike me, prairie born and bred, with a small-town view of the world.

I imagine Kathryn would have a fit if she heard me calling her a girl, for she is very much a woman, a focused woman—a corporate lawyer, in fact, with the suit to prove it. She is always telling me that I need to get more focused. But I am not focused. I am mostly depressed, a flat character, living in a flat world, as two-dimensional as the paper cutouts my girls used to play with.

It's difficult, sometimes, being the nobody husband of a corporate lawyer. I stay home with my girls—Stefanie and Bryanna—and pretend to write. I have three unfinished novels, two unfinished collections of short stories, and a good deal of poetry, which was me trying to find a way to write in a more sincere and focused manner. But I am not terribly sincere, and I am certainly not focused, as I said, although I did try. I even wrote some poems for Kathryn. It wasn't easy. What on Earth can you write for a corporate lawyer who lives her life with a cell in one hand and a coffee in the other, and who has sex with the same deliberateness with which she approaches her work?

Not that I'm complaining. My dad, a farmer who is the son of a farmer's son, could never understand why a woman like Kathryn would ever marry me, which for him meant that it was beyond him why a girl so smart and pretty would marry somebody like me. He said that to me once. Kathryn would, of course, object to being called pretty, but she might agree with him.

I can't say I really get it, either. Dad and Kathryn didn't like each other at first, but after sixteen years they have come to what seems a mutual understanding. Dad, with his bull-like, small-town belligerence, and Kathryn, with her polished certainty, have each managed to gain the other's grudging respect, mostly because of the kids. My dad dotes on his granddaughters.

Kathryn works long hours for this corporation while I look after Stef and Bree. I take time to write, which is what I call it, and Kathryn never gives me a hard time about what I do as long as the kids are fed and the house is clean. If I keep up my end of the bargain, then I'm not a liability, which is fine because I don't intend ever to be a liability.

I stand now at the kitchen counter slicing potatoes for dinner. The ham sits in a pan on the stove, and lined up against the back of the counter from left to right are the cheese, a grater, the milk, and a bowl for grated cheese. I am preparing ham and scalloped potatoes for dinner. Both my children are out—Stef at a friend's down the street and Bree at the mall with one of her girlfriends. Bree started junior high this year. I check one of the stickies lined up along the kitchen cupboards. Both kids are due back at five thirty. Kathryn isn't due home until six thirty. The television in the living room is tuned to CBC News World: first, for the sake of my stagnating brain, and second, so I'll have something intelligent to say to my wife after dinner besides commenting on how scalloped potatoes run over when you use white sauce but don't when you use milk. My wife follows the news; she knows what's going on in the world. I don't, but I'm informed enough to fake it.

It's not even five o'clock, but I'm ready for a scotch more than usual—a bad day. I spread sliced potatoes in the bottom of the casserole dish and decide that I will have a scotch, but not until dinner is in the oven, and only the blend, not the malt—as though this makes any difference. I convince myself it does.

I look up to scan the cupboard in front of me again. Anything I think I need to remember around the dinner hour I write down on stickies and put here on the cupboard above the stove. There are several. The one I want is when Kathryn will call. The one at the top says:

Kath—check in before five.

I return my attention to my potatoes. I, as you may have gathered, am a man of paper—of notes, sticky notes, actually. Here and there over the kitchen cupboards, covering the fridge, and plastering the board behind the table, are my notes, my sticky notes, in yellow, green, pale blue, and white. Notes to remind me of what I am doing from moment to moment, notes to tell me what to make for lunch, what to make for dinner, when to take out the garbage, what I need from the store, when to call my wife, when to expect my kids, what to think about tomorrow, what to remember from today. Notes, notes, and more notes, orchestrating my life, directing my thoughts, and reminding me to express those feelings I can't quite manage. I am a man whose life is held together by stickies. A paper man, whose life is fractured and reduced into short, cryptic notes on coloured bits of stationery, scattered over my house like outsize confetti.

After nearly eight years of being at home, I am a marginal success at being a stay-at-home dad, and a dismal failure at being a husband. I stopped wanting to have sex with my wife about two years ago. For a long time, I felt as though I was demanding something of Kathryn, which she was mostly too tired, or too uninterested, to give. And then I simply stopped wanting her altogether, shedding my desire as easily as a ragged old coat. It simply didn't matter anymore, and, oh god, what a relief that was.

I didn't make a conscious decision to stop wanting Kathryn, but I do remember the night when it happened. We came home from a corporate gig one evening on a weekend, a suit affair with glasses of wine and those little plates for hors d'oeuvres. It must have been in late spring because I remember Kathryn's dress. It was that midnight-blue thing slit halfway to her hip that leaves her arms and shoulders bare. She was prepared to go to the party as is, or was, but I insisted that she wear something over top because of the evening cool, and had to fuss over her for ten minutes before she would agree.

I go to these things as the husband of the corporate lawyer, and I've gone often enough for them to have blurred together in my mind years ago. These events are largely characterized by crystal on white tablecloths, with a lot of brass around, and punctuated by the occasional leather sofa or white carpet. I mostly remember a lot of shiny stuff. I would help myself to a glass of red wine while my brain registered voices, the closeness of people, the smell of the crowd, and then tried to remain genial, or the nearest approximation. Most of these suits did not know what to make of me. When asked what I did, I replied, with an appropriate gravity, that I was a writer, which isn't true, but contains enough of a truth to make me feel as though I'm not lying. When I tell the suit that I stay home and look after my kids, the feigned interest glazes over, and if I happen to mention that I don't drive a car, the look turns to blank surprise.

This particular occasion two years ago felt more than usually onerous. I don't remember why. I do know that the careful balance I had perfected between my depression and my exterior self was beginning to get shaky, and I could feel myself getting thin around the edges.

Not being able to stand the corporate chitchat, I made my way through talk of upsizing and downsizing and outsourcing and contracts to the coffee table, and welcomed the sight of a book that seemed to be about the Yukon territory. Perching myself on the edge of a couch that looked too expensive to sit on, I reached for the book and began flipping pages. I knew nothing about the Yukon, but I quite liked the photos of all that space. Thank god and Mel Hurtig for coffee table books.

"It's beautiful country," said a voice from somewhere above my head.

I looked up. It was my hostess, somebody or other's wife, whose name in that moment I could not recall. "Yes," I said stupidly, "it's beautiful." And then, not knowing why I said it, "I worked up there one summer during university." This was a barefaced lie, but it just seemed to come out. I may have been thinking of my cousin, who, when I was a kid, went somewhere up north to work as a fishing guide.

"Oh," she said, looking at me with a mild sort of politeness, "and what did you do?"

I'm sure this woman was attractive. I couldn't make up my mind, or I didn't want to. She was standing too close to me; I could smell her deodorant working hard against the heat of the room and feel the fabric of her dress brushing against my knee. I wanted her to go away. "Worked at a fishing lodge," I said, and swallowed some wine, which I did not taste.

"Oh, and where was that?" she asked in that maddeningly polite tone, which was really beginning to get on my nerves.

"Up near…Carmacks," I concluded decisively. I think the wine was going to my head. I had no idea where Carmacks was. I had only ever heard the name in a Stan Rogers song and knew it was somewhere in the Yukon.

"Carmacks," said my hostess in a flat voice. She looked at me closely. "I grew up in Whitehorse," she said. "I'm glad you like the book." And then she glided away into a wall of bodies, leaving me sitting there with the book in my lap, an empty glass in my hand, and wondering what the hell had just happened.

Kathryn apparently wondered the same thing. After we got home, I settled the kids while Kathryn drove the babysitter home. I was sitting at the kitchen table with my book open when Kathryn came in. Not before she had taken a glass from the cupboard and had reached for the scotch bottle did she look at me. I knew something was coming.

Now, I have to tell you about my wife. She is beautiful—at least I think so. She is tall, fine-boned but muscular, with enough curve at waist and breast to make her very feminine. Her hair is dark, straight as a pin, and cut modestly about her shoulders, with pale, almost translucent skin, and clear eyes that are intensely blue and often implacable. I have seen the way she looks at people in the courtroom, and she was looking at me like that now.

Kathryn poured scotch into the glass. "Why did you tell Helen that you worked up at a fishing lodge near Carmacks one summer?"

I opened my mouth to say something, but no words came out. "Who the hell is Helen?" I finally managed.

Kathryn watched me closely, sipping her scotch. "Kevin's wife," she said coldly. "You know, the people's house we were at this evening."

I shrugged.

"Carmacks is on a fucking desert, for Christ's sake," she exploded. "If you're going to lie about something like that at least get your facts straight."

She was really pissed off. She stood there breathing and taking tiny sips of scotch, until finally setting down the glass on the counter.

"Perhaps you should see a counselor," she said in that tone which meant she had already made up her mind that this was exactly what I needed to do.

"A counselor," I said, feeling my face growing wooden. "Why?"

"Because. Depression has always been a thing for you, but it's getting worse. You haven't exactly been Mr. Fucking Sunshine lately, you know.

You need to do something about it—especially if you're going to start telling stupid lies like that. I want you to get some help."

I started to argue, but she cut me off.

"It's not so much the lies," she said (she was still mad). "It's that you just make shit up so easily."

I was taken aback. I wanted to say that making shit up was what I did. I was a writer. But I knew she wouldn't buy it—not then. "I'm not some kind of compulsive liar, Kath," I said, carefully, feeling the panic begin to rise in my throat, and wishing that I had her glass.

"I know, but I want you to get some help—please," she added, her eyes melting from glacial to rain-washed blue.

Not fair, going from corporate lawyer to entreating wife like that. But what was I supposed to do? On Monday morning, I picked a counseling service out of the yellow pages and phoned for an appointment. Then I wrote,

Date with a shrink
Thursday, 2:00

on a piece of green sticky paper and slapped it on the fridge. Thus began my life in stickies.

Back in the kitchen, I pour a scotch, having closed the oven on dinner, and stand back to observe my corner of the universe, where things like ham and scalloped potatoes can be predicted. It's just after five, and now all I need to do is wait for Bree and Stef.

I steel myself not to think about Bree at the mall. I have a problem with malls: the people, the mix of smells, the sense of being closed in all make me nervous. So when Bree asked earlier this year about going to the mall with her friends I said no. Kathryn, on the other hand, doesn't have a problem with malls, and when it came down to an argument between Kath and me about Bree going to the mall, I, of course, lost. You can't win an argument with a corporate lawyer, believe me—even if you share a bed with her. So Bree has taken to going to the mall at least once a week with her friends, and I stay home wondering when she'll get back and when I should start to worry. *Start* is probably the wrong word. I always worry.

I drink my scotch and observe the kitchen. There is an island in the middle of the floor. It holds the sink, a workspace, and a dishwasher beneath the workspace. Another argument I lost when we renovated the kitchen. The long counter to my left ends in the fridge, beside which is the microwave set on a wooden stand. To my right is the large, wooden kitchen table. Beyond the table is the living room. Out the window to my left I can see the yard, running down to the fence. It is November, and everything is a uniform brown, not a fleck of snow in sight. Too warm for November.

I am the most mediocre of fathers, but I do take a genuine interest in my children, even without my book—but I haven't told you about my book yet. Bree, the eldest of my children, is about to turn thirteen, although she sometimes acts twenty-one or five, depending on the day. The problem is that she is determined to acquire a woman's body, which has me disconcerted. At what point do I start worrying about boys? Stef, however, is ten and determined to remain a child, which is fine with me.

I set my scotch deliberately on the kitchen counter and walk into the living room. Again, the decor was not my idea, but I did draw the line at the leather sofa. How is a person supposed to nap on a leather sofa, for Christ's sake?

Tucked into a corner is a desk, and I find my book lying open in the middle of a carefully arranged collection of bills and other papers. I remember now that I was writing in it earlier this afternoon.

My book is a leather-bound folder I bought just before I gave up on the last psychologist. Her name was Joan—the psychologist, I mean—and she was so goddamn earnest it just about drove me crazy. I bought the book on her advice. My book is a record of my feelings. Scrawled over the pages, slanting this way and that, are short notes and phrases expressing those thoughts and feelings I know I need to remember.

On the first page of my book is a quotation from Hardy. I like Hardy, but not many people do. Joan, my everlasting earnest psychologist, suggested that I write something uplifting on the first page, so that when I open my book it will be the first thing I see. The quotation I picked is from *The Mayor of Casterbridge*, the last line, or most of the last line of the book:

"…*happiness was but an occasional episode in a general drama of pain.*"

I admit it's a little heavy-handed, but I've always liked it. My psychologist wasn't impressed. She blinked a lot when I read it to her.

If you get past the first page, then you will see short messages placed at random over the succeeding pages.

I love my wife. (I do love my wife; I just have to remind myself that I do.)
I am determined to heal. (From what, I'm still not sure.)
I feel certain my writing will go forward. (That's a lie.)
My children are a joy to me. (This one is true.)
I hate my parents. (Had to include that one.)

Most of these are here because I have to remind myself that I feel this way. And I do have feelings, just in case you were wondering. Feelings for me are like sounds you hear outside the house on a quiet morning—muffled and far away. By the way, I don't hate my parents; I just put it there to show Joan. She didn't like it. Perhaps she thought I wasn't taking this task seriously. My wife says that, too, that I don't take things seriously. But I do, especially my children.

The page facing me is dedicated to my wife. *Remember to be strong and supportive* is crossed out, and beneath it is, *she pisses me off*, which I had written this afternoon in a fit of childish spite when I remembered what Kathryn had said about missing our movie tonight because of work. I'm not really upset with her, but I remind myself that I should be; otherwise, I'll forget, and Kathryn will accuse me of being cold and distant, which of course I'm not. I look over the desk for stickies, and make a brief note:

Stay on your side of the bed.

I date it November fourth and stick it to the top of the page. Flipping through, I see that both Bree's and Stef's pages are nearly full, and I make another note, reminding myself to start new pages for both of them. On Bree's page, between *I love you forever* and *you are my darling*, I squeeze in *I will try to let you go, if I can.* This genuinely makes me feel a little sad. Ernest Joan informs me that part of my difficulty is not being able to name my emotions. I can name them fine; I just have to remind myself while I'm in the fog that I have them.

Except for my kids. I am aware lately that my girls are growing up, which I'm not quite able to deal with. When they were little, we spent many hours sitting and reading together, or wrestling on the floor, while they shrieked as I hung them upside down by their feet. I can't do that anymore.

It makes me sad. I've been at home and caring for them for the past eight years, after I lost my job and Kathryn got hers, so the thought of Bree growing up is wrenching.

I pick up my book and prepare to take it back to the kitchen when the phone rings.

Kathryn.

"Hey, Kath," I say, before hearing a voice.

"Kids?" she says. This is Kathryn's verbal shorthand for *where are the kids, and did you feed them?*

"Should be back soon," I say, glancing first over at the counter where my scotch is out of reach and then flipping back to Kathryn's page in my book.

Endearments.

"Did you want them to call when they're back—love?" It's not that I find endearments that difficult, but Kathryn can be forbidding when she's in corporate mode, and she's always in corporate mode when she calls from the office.

"No, that's okay. I'll see them when I'm back. And," she pauses significantly, "I can't get away until after nine."

"So you won't be home for dinner?" Sometimes I have to state the obvious.

"No."

"Fine," I say, reaching for stickies.

"I'm sorry," she is saying as I write,

Kath—back after 9:00.

"This contract will take me the rest of the week, and then things will settle down again."

"That's fine, dear," I say. The contract in question is some huge job that the corporation is vying for, and Kathryn, of course, is one of the people responsible for it.

There is a pause at the other end of the phone. "I'm sorry about tonight," she says, her voice dropping out of corporate and into wife.

My skin twitches, and I grip the phone. "It's all right," I say again. "I'll see you tonight."

Replacing the phone, I walk across to the kitchen counter and pick up my scotch. A careful sip, and then I remove one sticky from the cupboard and put the other in its place. I don't know why I am so rattled. It's not like this sort of thing doesn't happen regularly; it's the price I pay for being married to a corporate lawyer.

I finish my scotch and reach for the bottle in the cupboard. I pour a larger shot than the first, and this time leave the bottle on the counter. I look at the clock again—almost quarter past. Then I take my scotch, my book, and myself to the kitchen table and sit down.

It hasn't always been like this between Kathryn and me. For several years it was pretty good, really. But as my depression grows worse, so does my relationship with my wife, and the less we have sex, the more she works—or maybe it's the other way around. Shedding my desire two years ago didn't mean we stopped having sex, but the liberating thing was that I was no longer a slave to my own need. If Kathryn wanted to, I generally could, but I felt no compunction to do so, and certainly left her free to make the decision whether we did or not. This seemed to me a reasonable arrangement. Passive, true, but effective.

In the years of raising small children, I met a lot of women raising kids of their own, and the sexual needs of their husbands seemed to be the greatest imposition for each of the women I met. *Everybody wants a piece of me*, I remember one woman saying, as I sat around with a group of women, at least half a dozen of whom were breast-feeding. There's nothing like sitting around with a bunch of nursing mothers to change a guy's attitude toward his own desire.

The odd thing was, because I was raising small children as well, I understood what that woman meant, and for a time I even felt that Kathryn and I were allies or something. I was elated. I finally understood why my wife wasn't all that interested in being my wife. We were no longer husband and wife; we were comrades in the battle against raging male hormones. But it didn't last. Eventually, my depression got the better of me, and the lines once again blurred between my inadequacy as a husband and my wretchedness as a human being. So you can see why it was such a relief to lose my desire.

I sip scotch and turn pages in my book. I suddenly flip back to Kathryn's page and carefully write,

Make an extra effort to talk.

It's not as if I don't care; I do. But lately, I've noticed that there is a silence that hangs between Kath and me. I don't know what it is, but it makes me nervous, and today, being the kind of day it is, I am more anxious about it than usual.

This morning was an example of that silence. Kath was standing in the bathroom doing her makeup in front of the mirror. She was partly dressed—just bra and nylons—and leaning with one hip against the counter carefully applying eyeliner. Seeing her like that, the curve of hip and buttock clearly outlined, and the slight pinching of skin caused by the waistband of her panty hose, made me feel a distinct pressure in my chest. The bathroom is off our bedroom, and I stood just outside the door looking in.

She glanced over at me, one eye made up and the other not. "Something up?" she asked.

Some women would look freakish half made up like that. Not Kath. I felt my skin give a twitch, as it does when anxiety is taking hold, and I shook my head. "No," I said.

She turned her attention back to the mirror. "I'm going to have to go back to work tonight after dinner," she said, "so maybe we could watch that movie tomorrow night."

Not how I wanted to start my day. "Sure," I said. I was struggling to assert my exterior composure. I glanced back into the bedroom for something—I don't know what—but nothing presented itself. I found no ready response, and the silence hung in the air between us.

"You all right?" asked Kathryn, looking at me again.

"Fine," I said. "I'll get you coffee."

That's how I started my day. And now, Kathryn probably won't get home until after the kids are in bed. It may not seem like much, but if you're someone like me who lives on the edge of depression all the time, then the slightest thing can make for a bad day, and this is turning into a bad day.

I flip to a new page in my book. I write:
I will get through this day.

And then the phone rings, causing me to jump. I suck in my breath in an attempt to calm myself as I scramble up from the table and grab the phone, not knowing who in the hell it might be.

"Hi there," says a cheery voice. "It's Cheryl from down the street calling. Is that girl of mine over there?"

Girl of mine?

My mind has gone blank. "Sorry, Cheryl," I say, trying for time.

"Carrie and Bryanna were supposed to come here after the mall, but they never showed."

Oh shit, the mall.

"They're not back yet," I say evenly. "I was expecting them at five thirty."

"Really? Carrie said they'd come back here at five."

Fuck.

I'm looking desperately at the board for something to tell me what's going on. "Well, Cheryl," I say in an equally cheery voice, while a sickening buzz starts in my head, "Bree told me they would come back here at five thirty." This is singularly unhelpful.

"Oh, I'm sure somebody just got their wires crossed," says Cheryl. "Probably me. Just send Carrie home when she gets there." And then she hangs up.

I can't believe it. I stare at the phone for a second and then put down the receiver. What if they aren't back by five thirty? Who is going to go look for them? And where the hell would we start, anyway? Maybe I'm overreacting, but I don't think so.

In my head I can hear myself on the phone again with Cheryl and explaining for the fortieth time that, no, I don't drive, and could either her or Chuck go and look for the kids? I look at the clock on the stove—nearly twenty-five past five. Where in the hell are they?

It's moments like this when I am fully aware of my own impotence in the face of a crisis. I feel powerless to do anything.

Grabbing the bottle of scotch from the counter, I sit down at the table and look at my book. I write:

I am afraid. I don't know where my girl is.

I wish I could drive. I could hop in my car, like one of those detective guys on TV, and just take off. Those guys don't even have to carry their keys; the goddamn things are always sitting in the ignition.

But I don't drive—or, more accurately, I can't. It's not for some physical impairment, or even for lack of trying; I'm just simply too afraid to get behind the wheel. I'm okay with flying—figure that one out—but I can't drive a car. You should have seen earnest Joan with that; she really thought she had something.

But seriously, I can't drive a car because I'm scared shitless. When I was twelve, my dad nearly killed me the first time he tried to teach me to drive the pickup. We were in the middle of a fucking pasture, and I lost it when he tried to make me drive the truck across the field. I nearly ran over one of the cows. He was so mad he made me walk back to the house.

I look down at my hands, and I find that I have poured more scotch into my glass. A gap. When the hell did I do this? Am I getting drunk? The back door bangs, and I give a convulsive jerk, sloshing scotch onto my book. Mouthing bad words, as my kids call them, I get up and hurry across the kitchen to the back door.

It's Stef. She is standing on the landing, peeling off her coat and kicking off her runners. "Hi, Dad," she says. "Can I watch TV?"

"Have you seen your sister?" I ask. A stupid question, and it gets an appropriate look.

"I was at Michaela's. Can I watch TV?"

"Fine," I say, and she heads off down the stairs to the playroom.

I return to the kitchen and look at the oven. The dinner. When did I put it in? I grab oven mitts from the top of the microwave, clumsily pull out the scalloped potatoes, and set them on top of the stove. I check them. Not done. Need at least another thirty minutes. I look again at the clock. Five thirty. I have to do something.

I walk over to the table, close my book, and grab my scotch. I drain the glass and set it on the counter. Then I head for the door.

Shoes and coat, and then downstairs to talk to Stef. She is sitting on the couch watching TV. "Stef," I say, putting one hand on the door frame. "I'm going to go and see if I can meet Bree coming back from the mall." I am feeling unsteady, and the buzzing in my head is louder.

Stef looks at me, her eyes getting round. "She's not home?" she says.

"No. I think they're on the way back, but I'm going to see if I can meet them."

"Okay, Dad." She switches her attention back to the screen.

Upstairs, I lock the back door and head outside. It's dark, but unseasonably warm. November is supposed to be cold. I hurry around to the front of the house and try to remember which way Bree and her friends come home from the mall. It's hard to think; my brain is slow.

I hurry down the sidewalk and turn left. Our house is just off the main street which runs past the school, and I'm praying that Bree and Carrie are coming back the same way the kids and I have always come back from the mall.

But my brain is not working properly. It's thick and slow, and I am mostly conscious of my breathing. Across the street to the school, and I am heading toward the mall. Past the island where the kids play ball in the summer, and around the corner and across another street. No sign of them.

I can't imagine what's happened to them; I don't want to imagine what's happened to them. I breathe and breathe, and breathe again. What if I missed them? What if they decided to go the long way past the church? How am I going to find them?

I should have called Cheryl before I left the house. I should have called Kathryn. Why the fuck don't I carry a cell phone?

And then, I'm across the street from the mall. I hurry through the grass to the crossing, trying not to run. Traffic—bloody traffic. It seems to take forever to cross the street, and then I am half running across the parking lot, heading for the door.

The air of the mall hits me as I yank open the door, and I gasp, feeling momentarily dizzy. What the hell is happening to me? Inside. Now what?

They could be anywhere, or I might have missed them. I walk inside quickly, feeling sick at the smell of cinnamon buns and stale air. The mall divides here, but which way should I go? If I go toward the CD store, I can also check the food court. But what about that earring place—what the hell is it called?

CDs, I think, and turn left. People shopping, carrying bags, concentrating on themselves, not looking where they are going. More people, music, Christmas lights, for Christ's sake. Where the hell is my daughter?

I duck into the CD store, nearly knocking over a woman as I do so. I mutter an apology and look around. No Bree.

I leave and head for the food court. I can't see her, and I know this is entirely futile. People are looking at me strangely, but I don't care. I just want to find my kid.

Somebody is saying something that I can't quite understand. It's a moaning, breathy sound, and I realize in a dim way that it's me. Someone grabs my arm.

"Sir! Are you okay?"

I look up, and it's some guy wearing a uniform of some kind. Is he a cop? I don't know. "My daughter," I gasp. And I realize I am crying.

"Your daughter," he says, frowning slightly. He has dark hair, and I can see through the blur that his nostrils are flaring as he looks at me, his eyes at once critical and compassionate. "How old is she?" he asks.

But I shake my head, and head back down the mall corridor. The tears are streaming down my face, and I don't understand why. I ignore them and wipe at my face in order to see clearly. No Bree.

At some point before reaching the door where I'd entered, it occurs to me to phone home. I fumble in my pockets for change, and finally dig out a quarter. I punch the number, make a mistake, and try again.

"Hello," says a voice.

Bree.

"Bree," I say in a half whisper.

"Dad," she says. "Where are you? I got home a few minutes ago, and Stef said you went looking for me."

"Yeah, sweetie," I say, slumping against the phone. "I thought I could meet you coming back."

"I'm sorry, Dad. We decided to take the bus, and then we missed our stop, so we had to walk back through Mich."

University housing, my brain registers. Opposite direction. "It's okay, sweetie," I say. "And Carrie?"

"She went home."

The buzzing in my head subsides a little, and I feel a flat wave engulfing me, leveling out my world and everything in it to a uniform gray. "I'm at the mall. I'll be home soon. Please turn off the oven for me. Your mom won't be home until late. We'll eat as soon as I'm back."

"Okay," she says. "Bye, Dad."

I put the receiver back onto its cradle with the deliberate, unconscious motion of a sleepwalker. I turn for the door and head outside. The air revives me a little as I make my way across the parking lot and the bus terminal, and wait for the light to cross the street. It's unseasonably warm for November. Cutting across the space of grass that separates the street from the alley and the backs of the houses, I glance up to a sky where the only light is that of streetlamps reflected upward into a nondescript glow under lowering cloud. The thought of home spurs me on—supper, dishes, kids, my wife, and the endless notes that orchestrate and organize my life. A paper man, a pathetic man, void of feeling, void of desire, with nothing but stickies, endless stickies between me and the truth that so terrifies me. Perhaps if I had the courage…

THE TENT TRAILER

On a Monday evening in late October, a week after he retired from his job at the packing plant where he had worked for more than thirty years, my father went out to the garage and shot himself with a .22-caliber rifle.

At the funeral, and for weeks afterward, people—friends, neighbours, and even relatives—asked me again and again if I had known something was wrong. I always paused when asked this question. I would say that I had seen my dad just the week before. He seemed fine. People who asked this question always looked at me with a kind of pitying resolve, as if they knew that I was in some kind of denial, or as if they understood the position I found myself in as the adult child of a man who committed suicide.

But my father had seemed fine the week before, or at least he had not seemed any different from the way he'd been for as long as I could remember. People would nod or make sympathetic noises, inventing the story for themselves and speculating how well I had known or had not known my father. I could have told them that. I did not know my father well, but I knew him well enough—well enough, in fact, to know that he was one of those miserly people who hoards misery and bad feelings as his only way to spite the world.

My father and I came to what I later thought to be our first real understanding on the eve of the family holiday the summer before my tenth birthday. For the six of us who lived in the small house in Norwood, the family holiday was the one time during the year we were inextricably bound together for two full weeks. For the other fifty weeks of the year, including Christmas, we all went our separate ways: school for all of us, Little League in the summer for Danny and me, friends and half-mysterious pursuits for my two older sisters. My mother worked part-time at the Safeway, ran the house, and bullied us into going to church whenever she could—mostly at Christmas and Easter. Often, she looked tired. Seeing her that way gave me a curious hollowness in my chest, but I could never just go up to her and hug her the way Danny could.

For my father, the days must have blended into one another. He would get up at five thirty every morning, make his coffee on the gas range in the kitchen, fry his two slices of bacon and two eggs, and leave the house carrying his metal lunchbox for the job he hated. But every summer he would ready the old canvas tent trailer for the family holiday, painting the wooden box and doing minor repairs until the day the car would be packed to the windows with pillows and comics and coats, and we pulled away from the curb with the trailer following behind like an obedient puppy.

My father built that tent trailer with his own hands; that's what he always said—his own hands. He parked his car on the street for four months one year so he could use the garage to have the trailer ready for the family holiday in August. That's what he would tell people—that he had to park his 1965 cream-coloured Plymouth "on the street" so he could finish building the trailer in time for the family holiday.

I have only one memory of him actually building that trailer. It must have been nearly finished because in my memory I am kneeling on the concrete floor of the garage beneath one of the foldout wings. I must be at the back of the trailer because I do not remember the dark metal of the tongue. Metal supports like tent poles hold up the wing of the trailer, the poles set into chunks of two-by-four-like blocky, wooden feet. I am interested in something on the floor of the garage, but I am also aware of the sound of my father's breathing. He is working somewhere out of sight, but I can hear his breath coming hard, punctuated by short gasps and grunts, as though he is straining to fix something. Although I am not really aware of it then, I know now that this concentrated, frustrated ferocity is the way my father approaches any task. Anything that needs fixing he approaches with the same determination, and yet he always seems to perceive a broken item as a personal slight, as though the thing has deliberately stopped working because of who he is. Perhaps I am being too hard on him. He loved us all, I suppose—Danny the most. But of all of us I was the one to carry the burden of his anger, his guilt, and his self-reproach.

For most of the year, the trailer was parked at the back of the yard. Like everything that my father fought with and cursed, it took on part of his personality—a quiescent part of my father's rage.

I passed it every time I carried the garbage out to the back alley where I dumped the overflowing paper bag, soggy and smelly, into one of the three battered cans that stood against the fence. Snow piled around the trailer through the winter, until the dark metal tongue of the frame would be buried in snow and the canvas top thickly layered like frosting on a store-bought cake. When spring came, the snow would slowly melt to reveal the wet canvas that dried in the steadily increasing warmth of the sun. Then we would pile on top of the trailer, the canvas hot under our hands and its sharp smell in our nostrils.

But only in the spring would we climb over it. When summer came again, it took on the waiting expectancy of something about to be used. My dad would clean it off and touch up the wooden box with the gray, cement-coloured paint he kept on a shelf in the basement. He would then begin to fiddle with it: setting it up and taking it down, fussing with it and swearing at it, cursing it to hell every time something went wrong, until it was finally ready for the impending holiday.

Every year the holiday was different. We drove and camped, camped and drove, over flat miles of bald-ass prairie, and up and down foothills that undulated like the breath before sleep. Sometimes we drove high up into the mountains, one piling itself on the next, steep slopes sometimes bare and sometimes thick with trees, until the ground would open before us to reveal a stretch of water, silent and shining clearest blue or palest green. Once we got as far as Vancouver Island to visit relatives, where I was able to walk on the beach and stare at the alien water that ran out to the edge of the sky, the fish smell heavy in the air and the gulls—much bigger than the gulls at home—shrieking and turning on the wind.

"You have to fix the taillights on the trailer," my mother says one evening in early August. "We need to leave tomorrow. The only thing left to pack is the hamper. Everything else is done." She stands over the blue plastic laundry tub that she calls the hamper, filled with canned and packaged food for our trip: ham and spaghetti, boxes of crackers, and packages of macaroni and cheese. She is looking at my father over the hamper, and he is standing in the doorway of the kitchen, looking as though he wants to say something but can't.

I am coming up the basement stairs and see them standing like that. I stop with my foot on the top step. I stand suspended, holding my breath and watching my father for his reaction, waiting for him to do or say something.

"I'll have it fixed," my father says in that voice that I know is meant to goad my mother. "I know what the problem is. I'll get it done."

My father is incapable of simply talking. Everything is a confrontation that requires all of his restless energy. I watch his hands.

"Then why isn't it done? If you can't fix it, then get some help. Ask Norm. I saw him in the garden just a few minutes ago. He was out there looking at the apple tree. He'll be happy to help. He's always wanting to help. Why don't you just let him?"

"I'm not going to ask Norm. He is a pain in the ass. I know he wants to help, but I don't want his goddamn help."

My mother notices me standing at the top of the stairs. I think she is glad to look away from my father. I can see the spots of colour in her face that appear whenever scenes like this begin.

She brushes at her hair with the back of her hand. "Well, don't just stand there. Bring me those cans."

Obediently, I take the last step and come into the kitchen, placing the cans into the laundry hamper. My father swings around and walks out the door, letting the screen slam behind him. The evening is warm, and I can hear the sounds of birds and the drone of an airplane outside the kitchen window. I look at my mother, but she is studying the list in her hand, a long cardboard sheet printed on and scribbled over with pencil. She is checking off the items on the list against what is in the hamper.

I want to follow my father, not because I don't want to help my mother, but because I believe that I can actually be of some help. I always think this, and I am always wrong.

My father is an angry man. He tries to keep his anger at bay, but it has a way of exploding through his moods and becoming destructive and hurtful. He does not hit me, but he hits Danny, my younger brother, but Danny never seems to care. Danny cries, certainly, but afterward he simply carries on with the next thing he is doing. Danny is always getting into trouble of some kind, either at school or just running wild through the neighbourhood. Once on a dare, he stole some chocolate bars from the Chinese grocery, and my father beat him with his belt—Danny howling and wailing bloody murder, and my father yelling and swearing until my mother stopped him. My father does not hit me, but I sometimes wish he would. He yells at me and usually swears. He tells me that I am irresponsible or stupid or goddamn useless. I stand and receive the verbal assault until he finally tires. He tires much quicker with Danny than he does with me. My father's penchant for creatively cursing serves him well, but his anger has a way of shutting even that off, so when he is reduced to simple obscenities and accusation, then I know I must try to get away.

Can you not think?
Did God not give you a goddamn brain?
What the goddamn hell were you thinking of?
Son of a bitch!
Son of a bitch!

My father's anger would eventually run down, and I would be allowed to leave or escape to my room. There I would sit, on my bed or on the back steps, feeling the numbness spreading through my body, the numbness that protects me from the worst of his anger.

I stand now beside the car, watching my father trying to get the taillights to work on the trailer. The trailer does not yet rest on the metal ball of the hitch; it is simply connected by the wires that are supposed to make the lights on the trailer go on and off. He is already swearing. I step up to the driver's door and look in. I see a red light on the dashboard. In some inexplicable way, I think that I see the problem where he doesn't.

I step into the car and pull the lever beneath the light. The car jerks forward. I look up in surprise to see the car rolling toward the wall of the garage. Between the front of the car and the wall of the garage is Danny. He stares back at me in what I now know is consternation, not moving but simply standing there as the car rolls toward him.

What I don't understand until later is that the red light is the indicator light for the emergency brake. Somehow I manage to find the brake pedal; I am able to do that much. I get out of the car. It has stopped. Danny is flattened against the garage, and the car seems poised against his midriff, gathering itself—or so it seems—to move forward and crush him into the wall.

My father brushes past me, and I see him lift Danny from between the car and the garage wall. Then he turns. In that moment, I do not understand the expression on his face—white, with red blotches around nose and eyes. He steps forward. He does not say anything. He hits me hard across the side of the head, knocking me down so I fall against the fender of the car. I lie there for a moment, feeling the gravel of the driveway pressing into my face and smelling the underside of the car. I feel disconnected from everything other than the pain in my head. When I manage to clamber to my feet, I can see my father's back as he bangs through the back gate and disappears around the corner of the garage. He has not said a word.

"You're stupid," is Danny's only comment. But I believed, even then, that he didn't really mind what happened. He would tell and retell that story to friends and relatives, elaborating and changing the details to suit his audience. Danny would tell this story because he likes to take risks, and just as much he likes to tell people about it.

This love for danger will eventually kill Danny in an alpine skiing accident twenty years later near Jasper, where he is buried beneath thirty tons of snow and rock. This is the accident for which my father blames me—not the time I nearly killed him driving the car on the family holiday, as Danny would always say. I was not driving the car, and we were not yet on the holiday, but I never corrected him. Danny was not killed that day, and for some reason my father never blamed me for what happened. But he wanted to. So when Danny died in the skiing accident near

Jasper, my father was finally able to vindicate himself and berate me for all my failings. It was no doubt easier to blame me than it was to deal with the death of his beloved son.

And now my father is dead, too. I am not especially shocked by how my father died. It seems fitting somehow that his last act would be to walk out to the garage—beside which the trailer has not stood for years—place the barrel of a .22-caliber rifle into his mouth, tasting the oily metal of the barrel on his tongue and breathing noisily through his nose while he reached down to press the trigger with the callused ball of his thumb. And I wonder, too, if this was his way of punishing the people who loved him, those people who put up with his shit for all those years. And, too, if in those last few seconds he was watching through the garage window, through the twilight of an October evening, to perhaps catch a glimpse of my mother or oldest sister passing the kitchen window. But it's there my imagination fails. And I'm left to wonder over the man I knew and didn't know, to look for the answers I need, to circle endlessly round until I arrive at the questions all over again.

AFTERWORD

In my days as a grad student—long, long ago—I wanted to write a collection of stories that centered on the town of Galahad. You should know that the province of Alberta does, in fact, boast a town of Galahad, and though I haven't visited, I was always struck by the name because of its connection to the Arthurian legends. I hope the people of Galahad, Alberta, forgive me for using the name of their town. My fictional Galahad is based on a real place—a different town—but the people who populate it are imaginary.

In the 1990s, I received an Alberta Arts Foundation grant to work on the earliest conception of this collection, but I didn't attempt to submit it for publication for at least a decade. Over the years, newer stories have found their way into the collection, and while they aren't strictly Galahad stories, most of them fit with my overall intent, which has always been to explore characters who confront the past in the midst of the present. I have always found the present to be tricky. Things resurface, intrude, demand attention, and the present is the only place where such flotsam can be sorted.

The Paper Man, the title story for this collection, became the anchor story about halfway through the process, which has spanned almost twenty years. I was in the middle of the January blues about a year after my kids and I moved from university housing into our own home. January in Edmonton can be a devastating time—the days are still short and the cold and snow can be oppressive. I was depressed and couldn't write. My children were, I think, watching TV in the basement, and I was getting dinner ready—ham and scalloped potatoes. I got dinner in the oven and then walked over to my desk in the living room. Feeling as though I wouldn't be able to write another word, ever again, I sat down at the computer and began describing what I had just been doing. I described a dad who was getting dinner ready for his daughters. It worked. In not very long I had *The Paper Man*—at least a rough draft. It became, and has remained, the cornerstone of the collection.

Stories for me often begin as images. The next step is finding the voice to describe the image. The original image doesn't always survive the writing and editing process, but usually the voice doesn't change. I originally wrote *My Brother's Keeper* from the blind brother's perspective—a blind man sitting alone in his room on the day he is moving to a nursing home. That didn't work. Once I switched to Robert's perspective, writing the story was straightforward. The image of the father carrying the body of Tiff down a muddy, steeply sloping drive was the beginning of that story. The image and the voice stuck.

Stories also enable me to sort out things I can't in my own life. I don't think my fiction is any more biographical than anyone else's, but it is a reflection of what my brain, in some primal way, is trying to process. I wrote *The Tent Trailer* over a period of about two years, from 2005 to 2007. My dad died in June of 2005 from an aortal aneurysm, and *The Tent Trailer* became more and more a story that was helping me to address my sense of loss and grief. In the fall, more than a year after his death, I was out for a walk in the late evening and thinking about *The Tent Trailer*. The story wasn't working somehow, and as I walked, I came up with the first line of the story. My dad did not commit suicide, but having the father in the story kill himself went some way to help me sort out my feelings about my dad's death.

Writing is all of these things, but mostly it's just hard work. The long, tedious, and exasperating process of editing and revising, and fixing the myriad minor errors strikes me as a form of masochism. Regardless, I keep doing it. I hope anyone reading this collection finds, at the very least, some entertainment in these stories. Reading, for me, has been a lifelong passion. My hope, in some small way, is to re-create my own reading experience for someone else.

WT, August 2014

Manufactured by Amazon.ca
Bolton, ON